EEK & ACK OOZE SLINGERS FROM OUTER SPACE

Librarian Reviewer
Allyson A. W. Lyga, MS
Library Media/Graphic Novel Consultant
Fulbright Memorial Fund Scholar, author

Reading Consultant
Elizabeth Stedem
Educator/Consultant, Colorado Springs, CO
MA in Elementary Education, University of Denver, CO

Graphic Sparks are published by Stone Arch Books,
A Capstone Imprint
1710 Roe Crest Drive
North Mankato, Minnesota 56003
www.capstonepub.com

Library of Congress Cataloging-in-Publication Data
Hoena, B. A.
    Ooze Slingers from Outer Space / by Blake A. Hoena; illustrated by Steve Harpster.
    p. cm. — (Graphic Sparks. Eek and Ack)
    ISBN-13: 978-1-59889-315-1 (library binding)
    ISBN-10: 1-59889-315-7 (library binding)
    ISBN-13: 978-1-59889-410-3 (paperback)
    ISBN-10: 1-59889-410-2 (paperback)
    1. Graphic novels. I. Harpster, Steve. II. Title.
PN6727.H57O69 2007
741.5'973—dc22   2006028027

Summary: Eek and Ack, the Terrible Twins from the Great Goo Galaxy, are at it again!
They make more plans to conquer Earth, but this time something sticky gets in the way.
And it has eyes! And feet! And it's got the bug-eyed brothers trapped on an asteroid!

Art Director: Heather Kindseth
Graphic Designer: Brann Garvey

For my nephews Ryan, Chase, and Carter,
here's another book to read on our camping
trips — just don't eat the snottle bugs!

Printed in the United States of America in North Mankato, Minnesota.
052016
009742R

EEK & ACK
OOZE SLINGERS FROM OUTER SPACE

by Blake A. Hoena

illustrated by Steve Harpster

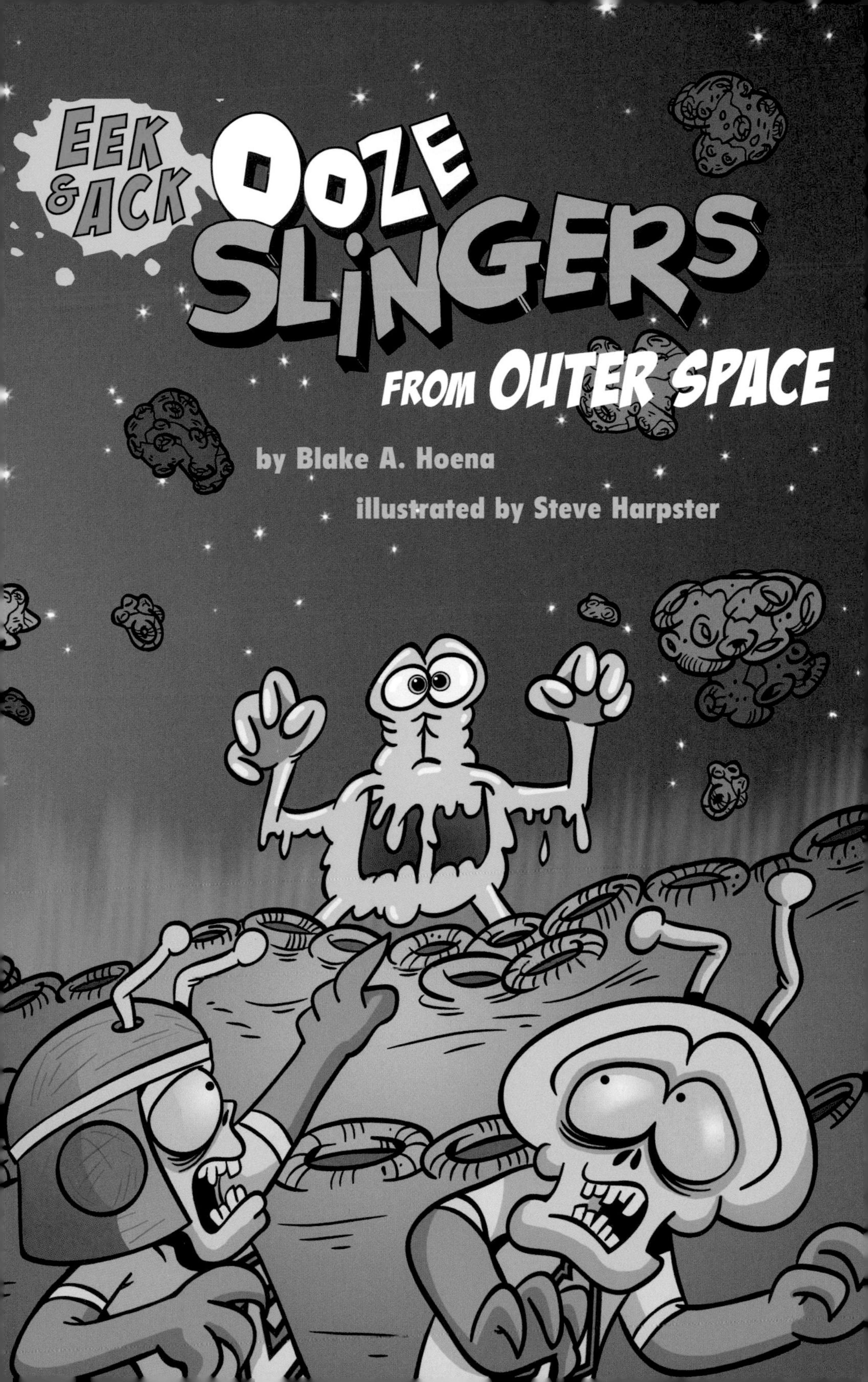

Cast of Characters

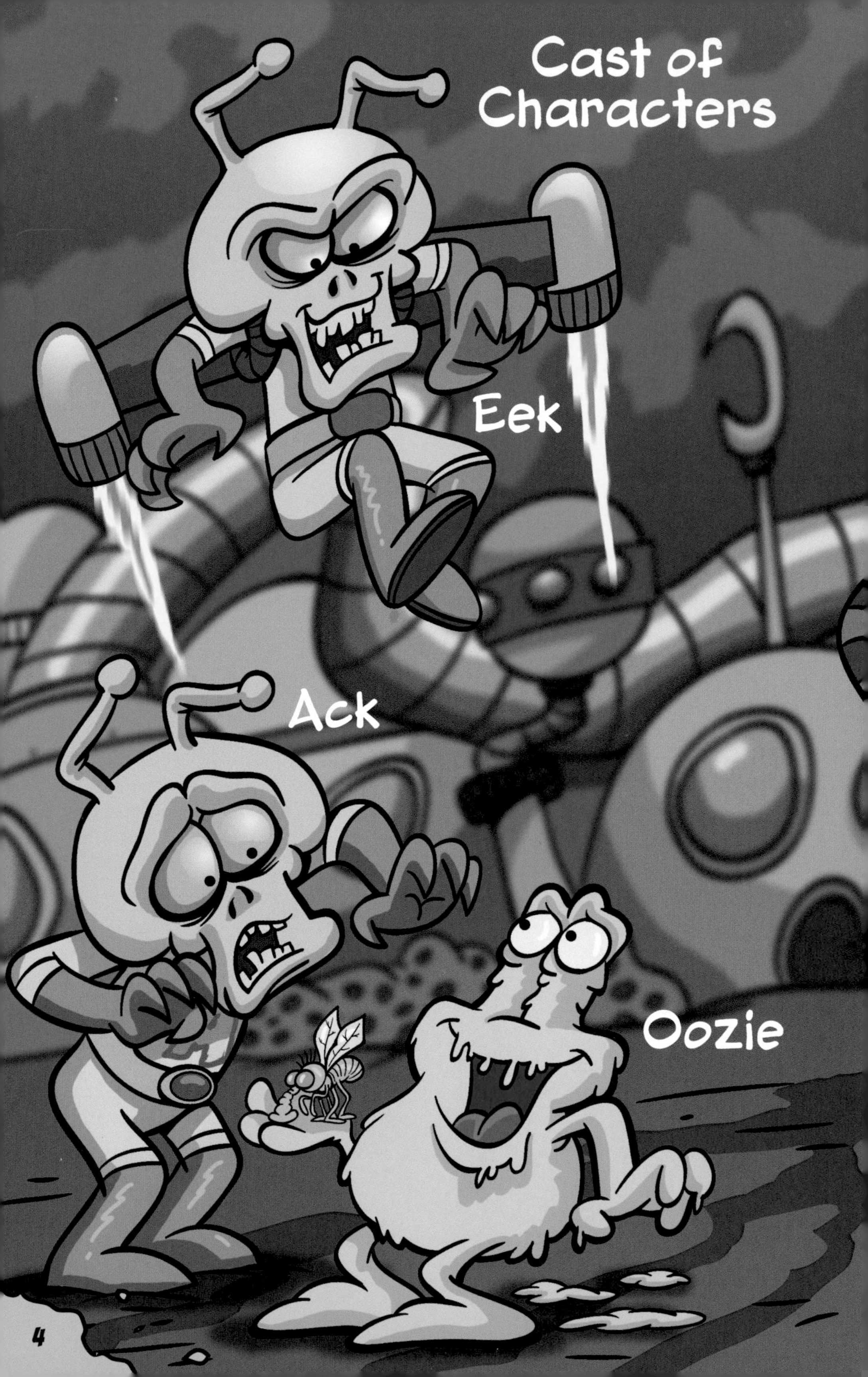
Eek
Ack
Oozie

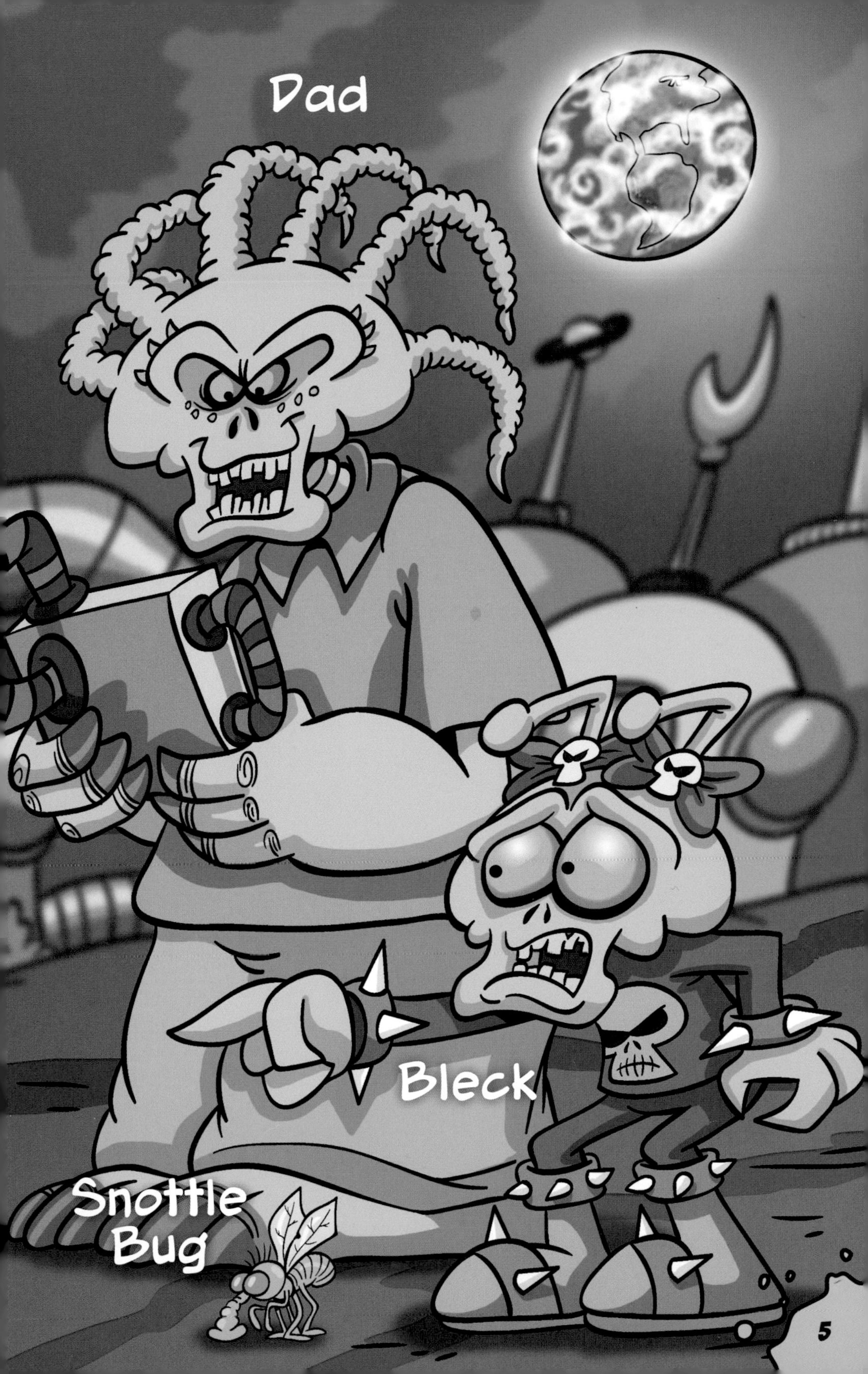
Dad
Bleck
Snottle Bug

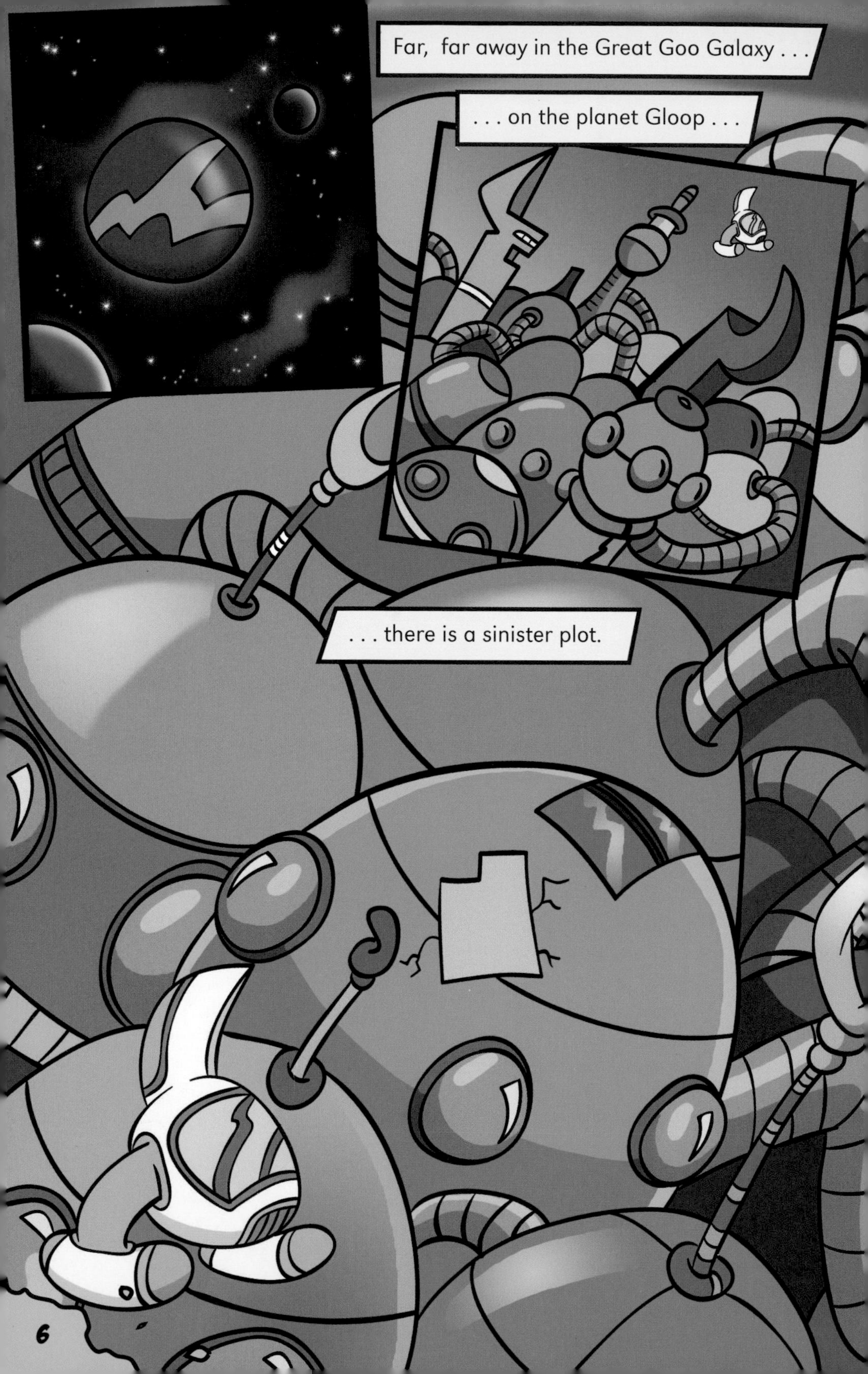
Far, far away in the Great Goo Galaxy . . .
. . . on the planet Gloop . . .
. . . there is a sinister plot.

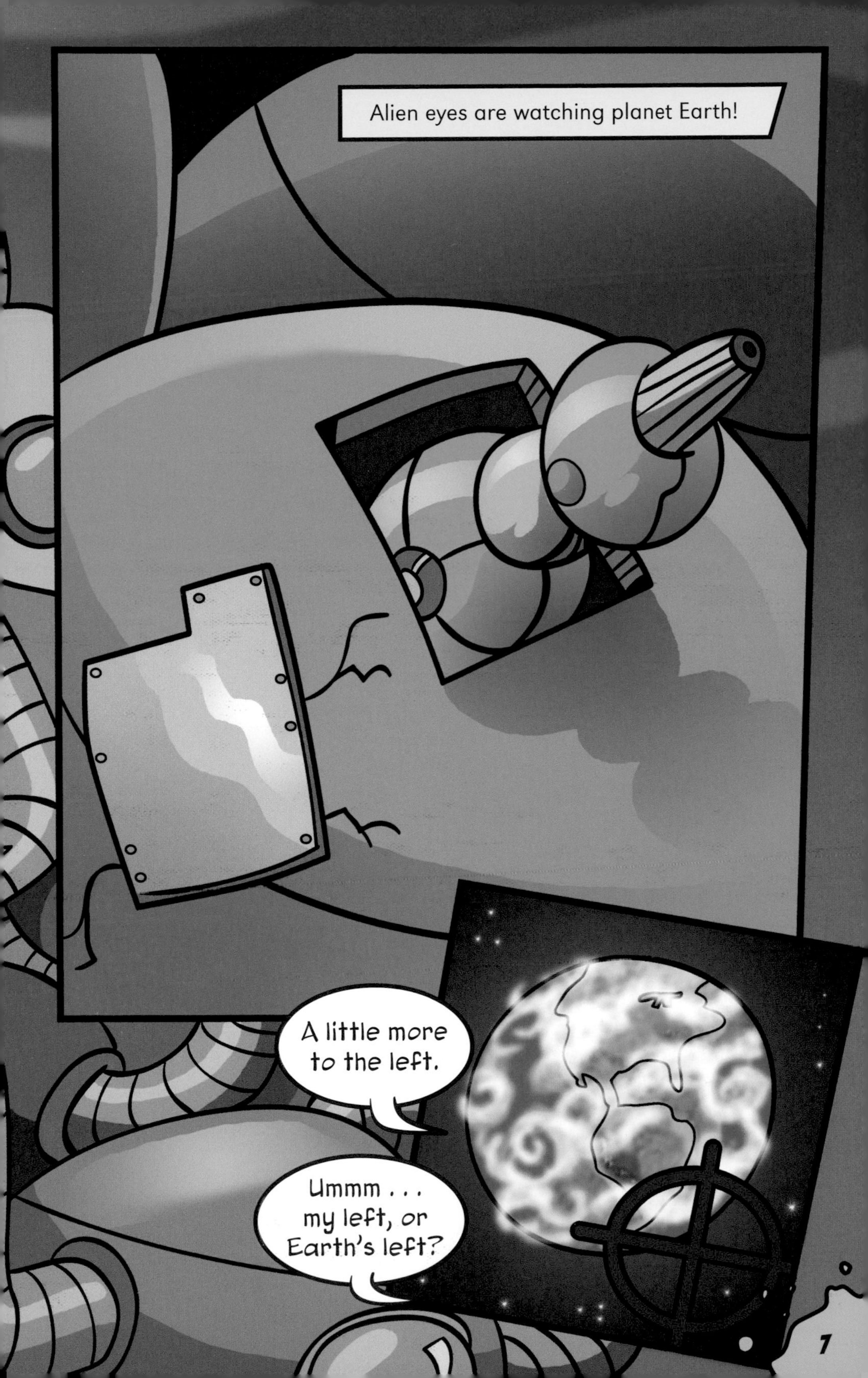
Alien eyes are watching planet Earth!
A little more to the left.
Ummm . . . my left, or Earth's left?

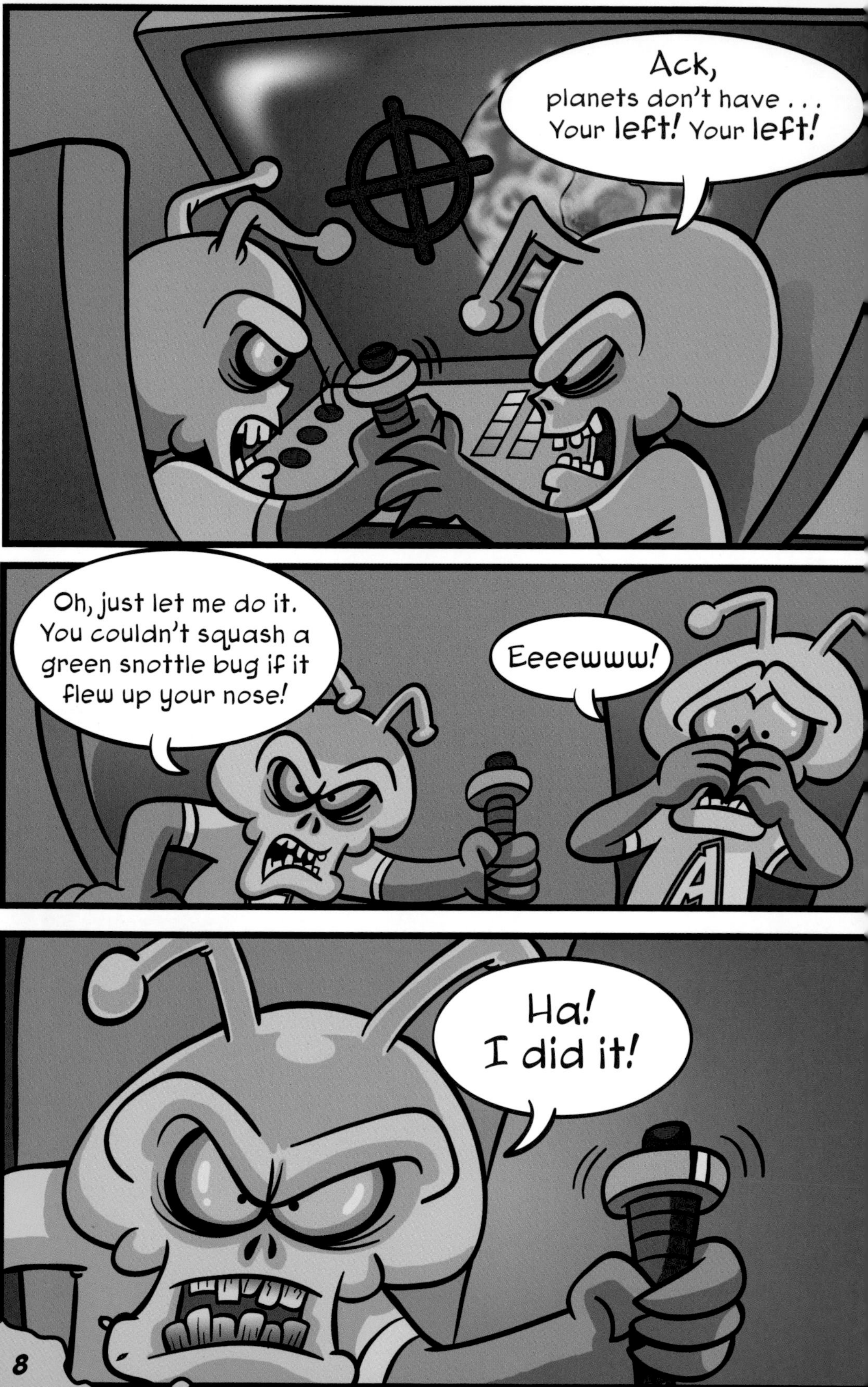
Ack,
planets don't have . . .
Your left! Your left!
Oh, just let me do it.
You couldn't squash a
green snottle bug if it
flew up your nose!
Eeeewww!
Ha!
I did it!

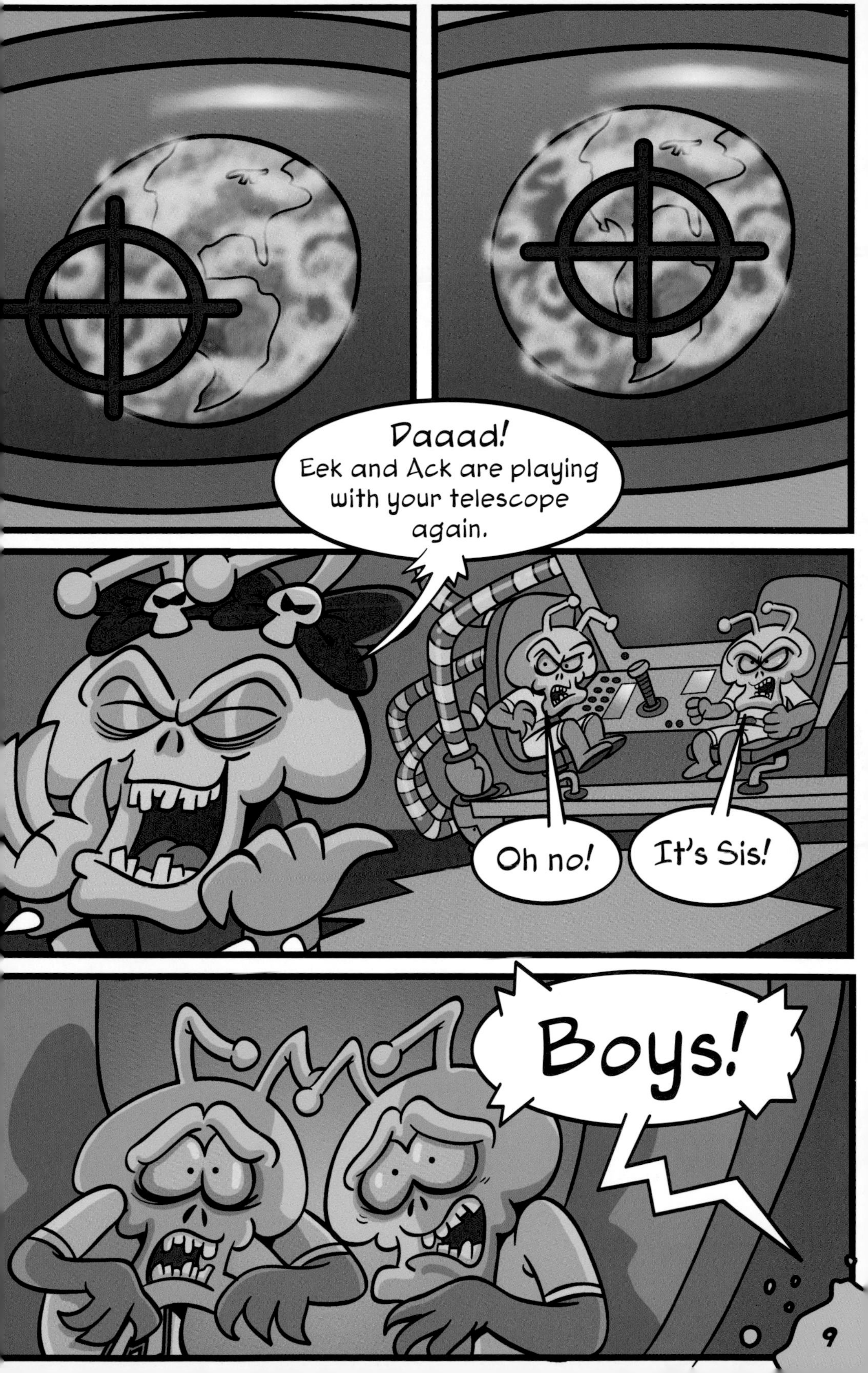
Daaad!
Eek and Ack are playing with your telescope again.
Oh no!
It's Sis!
Boys!

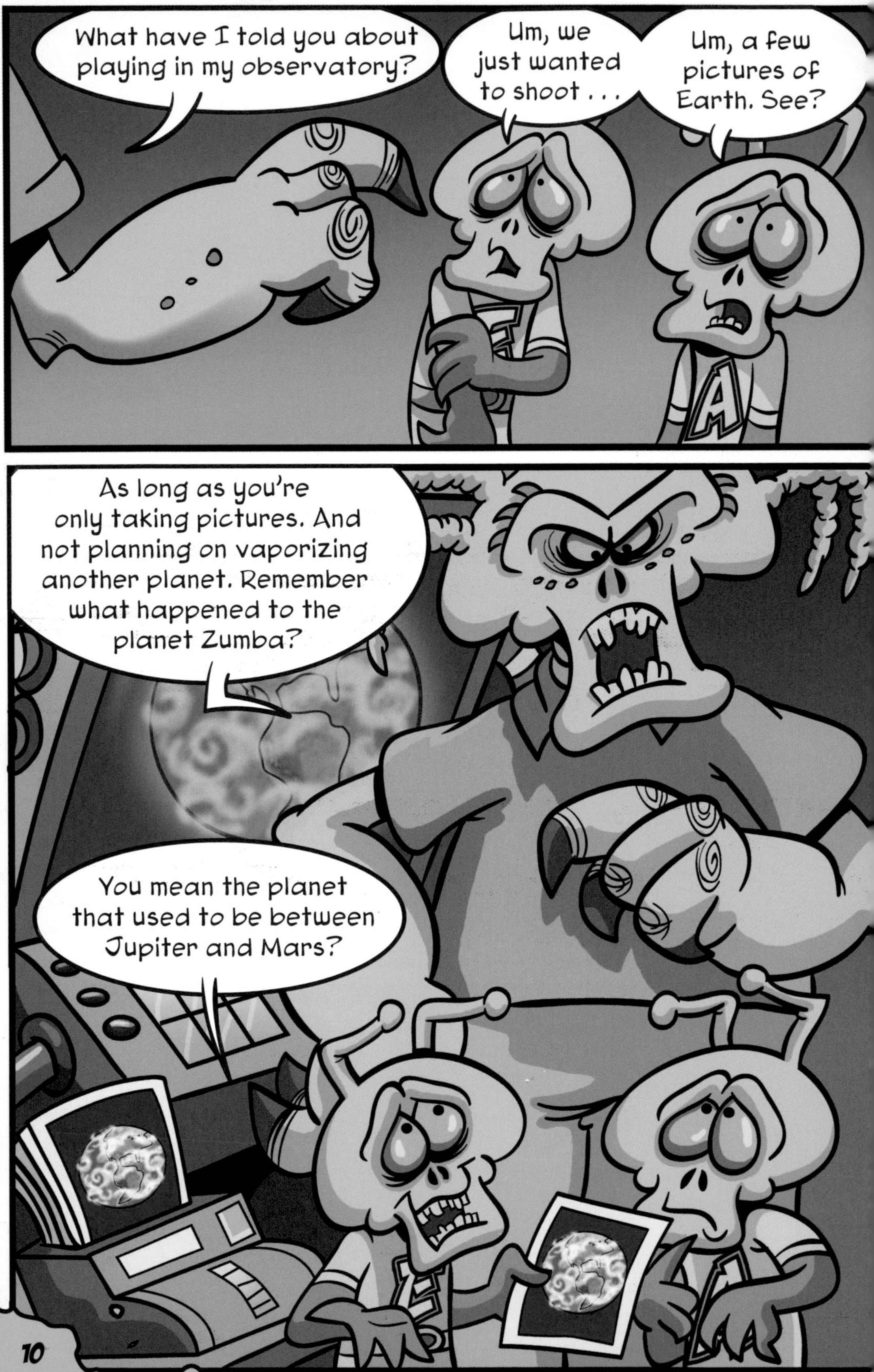
What have I told you about playing in my observatory?
Um, we just wanted to shoot . . .
Um, a few pictures of Earth. See?
As long as you're only taking pictures. And not planning on vaporizing another planet. Remember what happened to the planet Zumba?
You mean the planet that used to be between Jupiter and Mars?

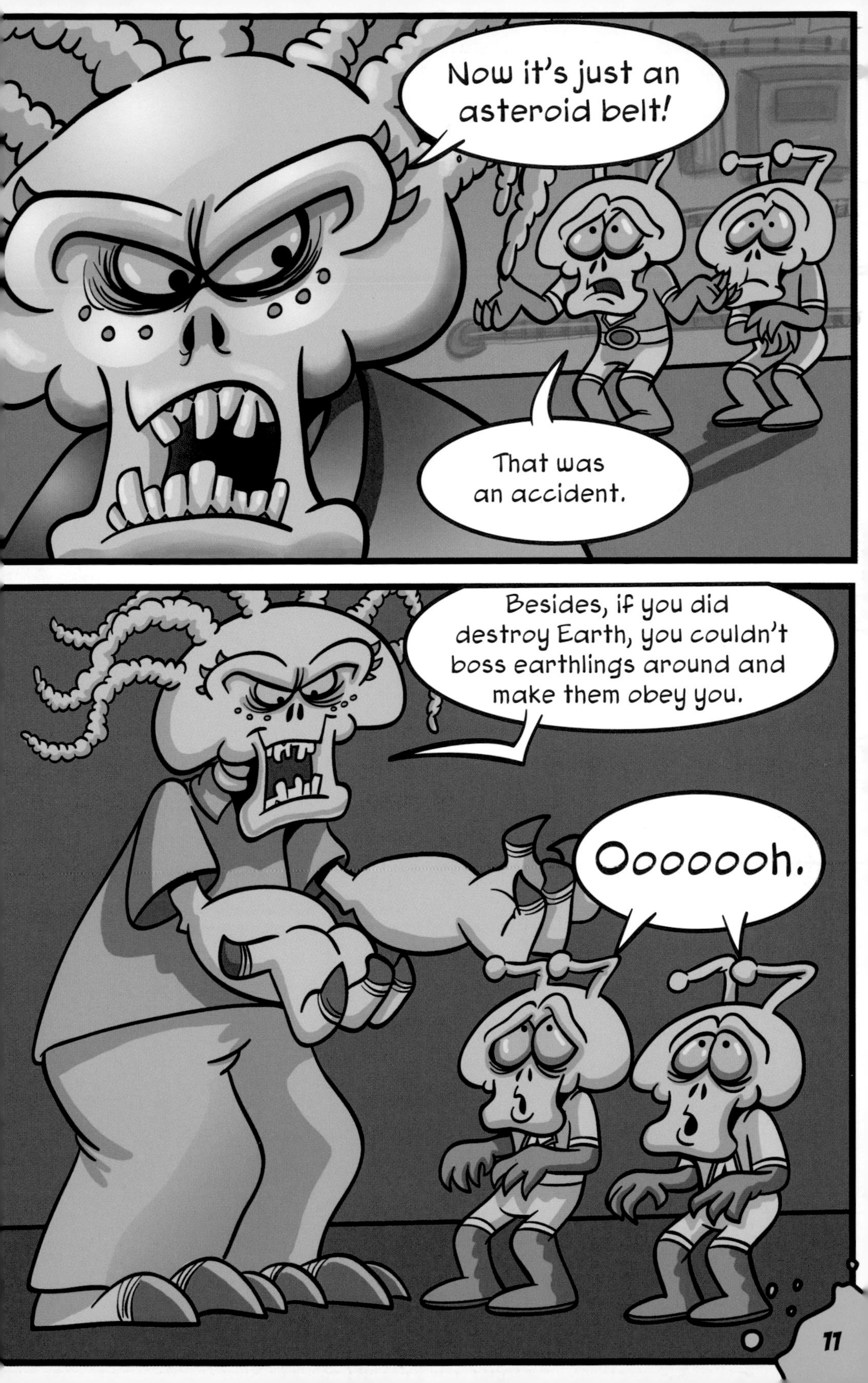
Now it's just an asteroid belt!
That was an accident.
Besides, if you did destroy Earth, you couldn't boss earthlings around and make them obey you.
Ooooooh.

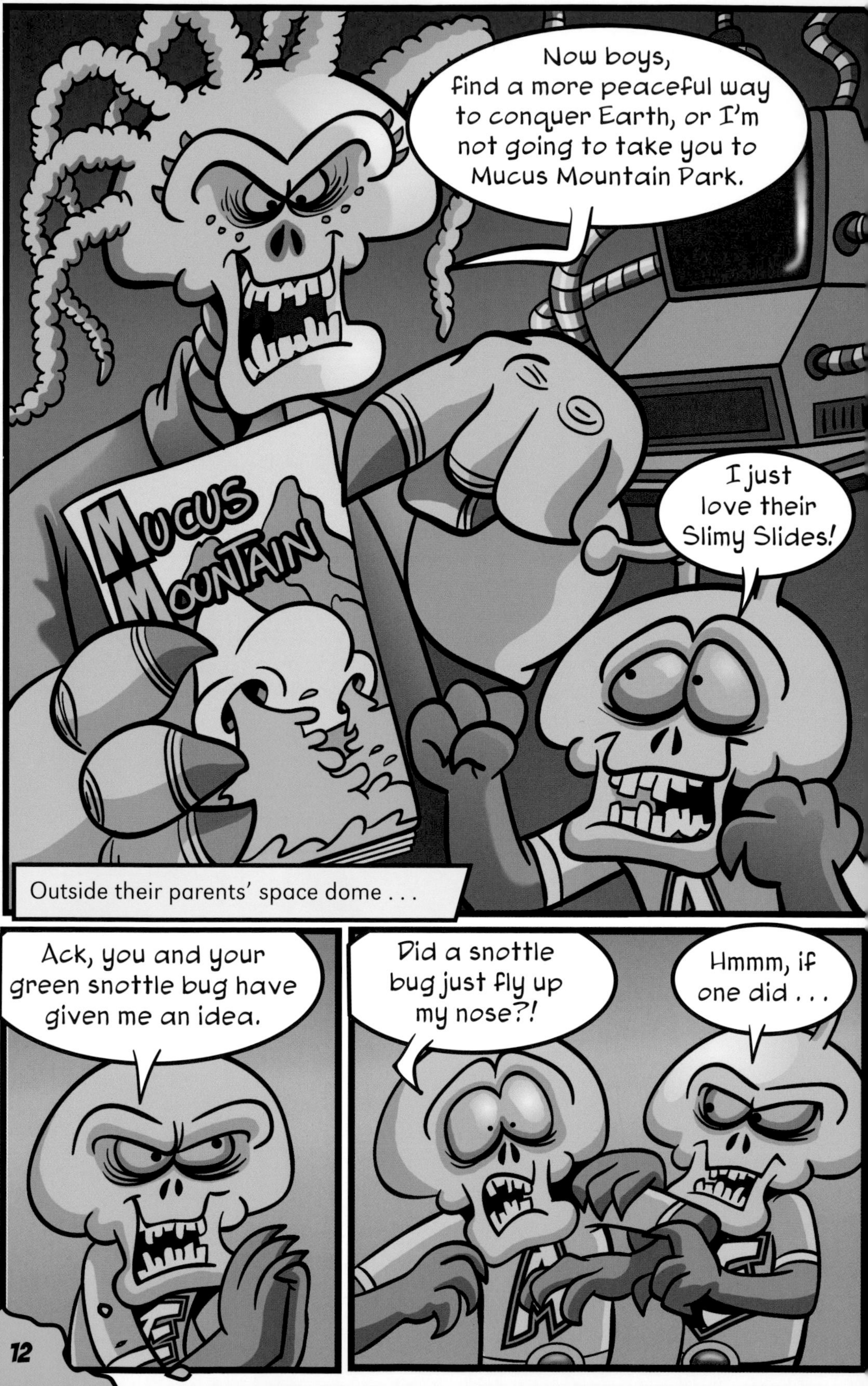
Now boys, find a more peaceful way to conquer Earth, or I'm not going to take you to Mucus Mountain Park.
MUCUS MOUNTAIN
I just love their Slimy Slides!
Outside their parents' space dome . . .
Ack, you and your green snottle bug have given me an idea.
Did a snottle bug just fly up my nose?!
Hmmm, if one did . . .

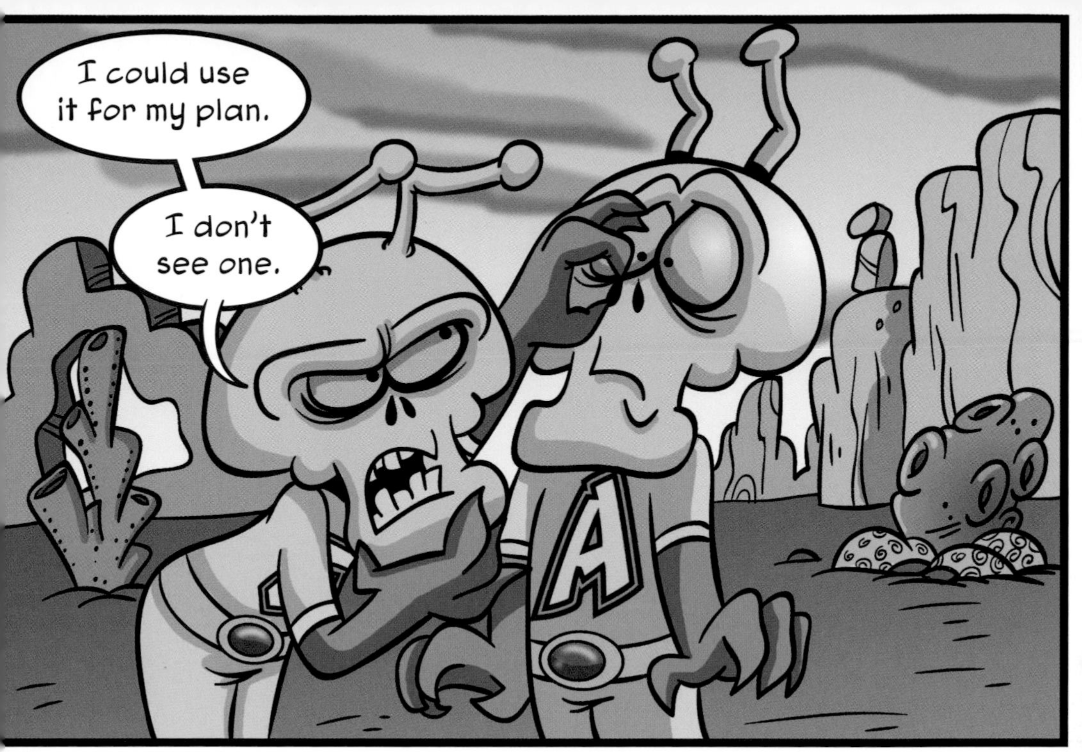
I could use it for my plan.
I don't see one.

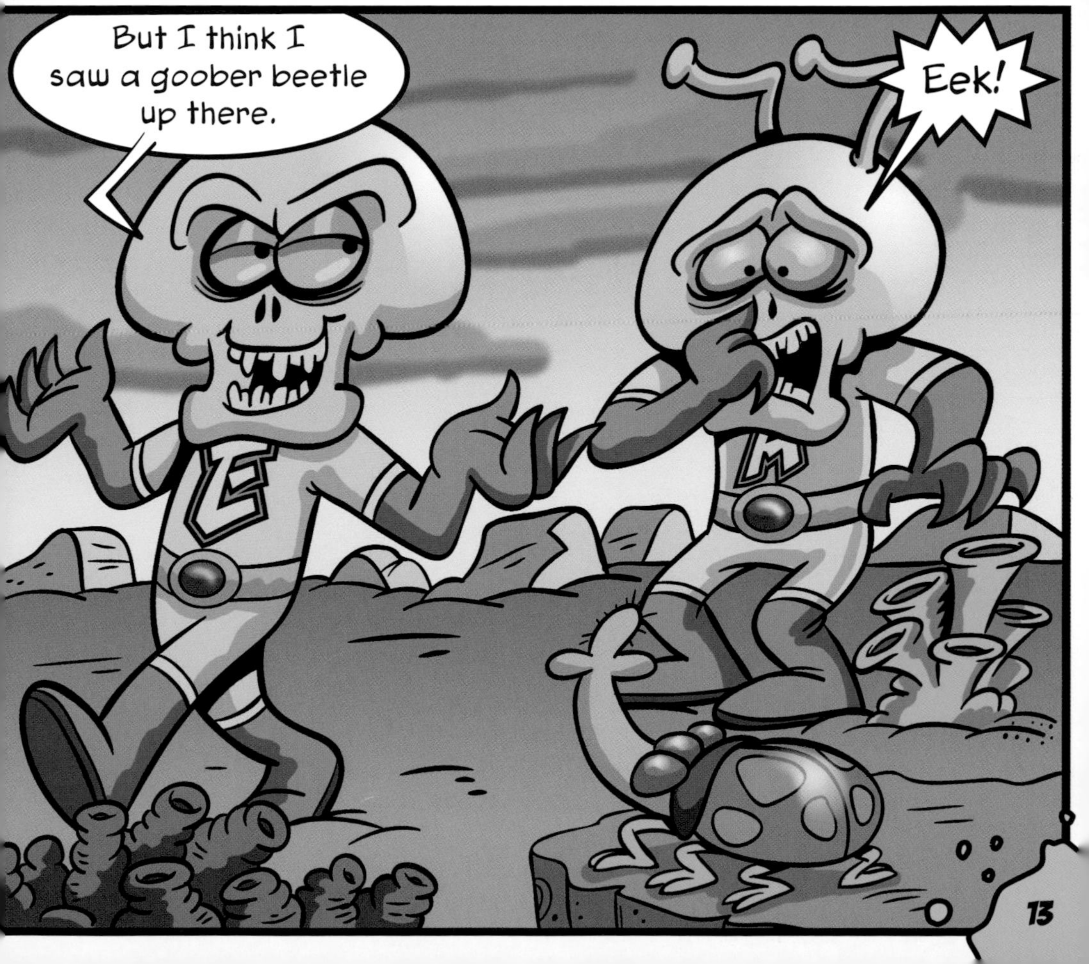
But I think I saw a goober beetle up there.
Eek!

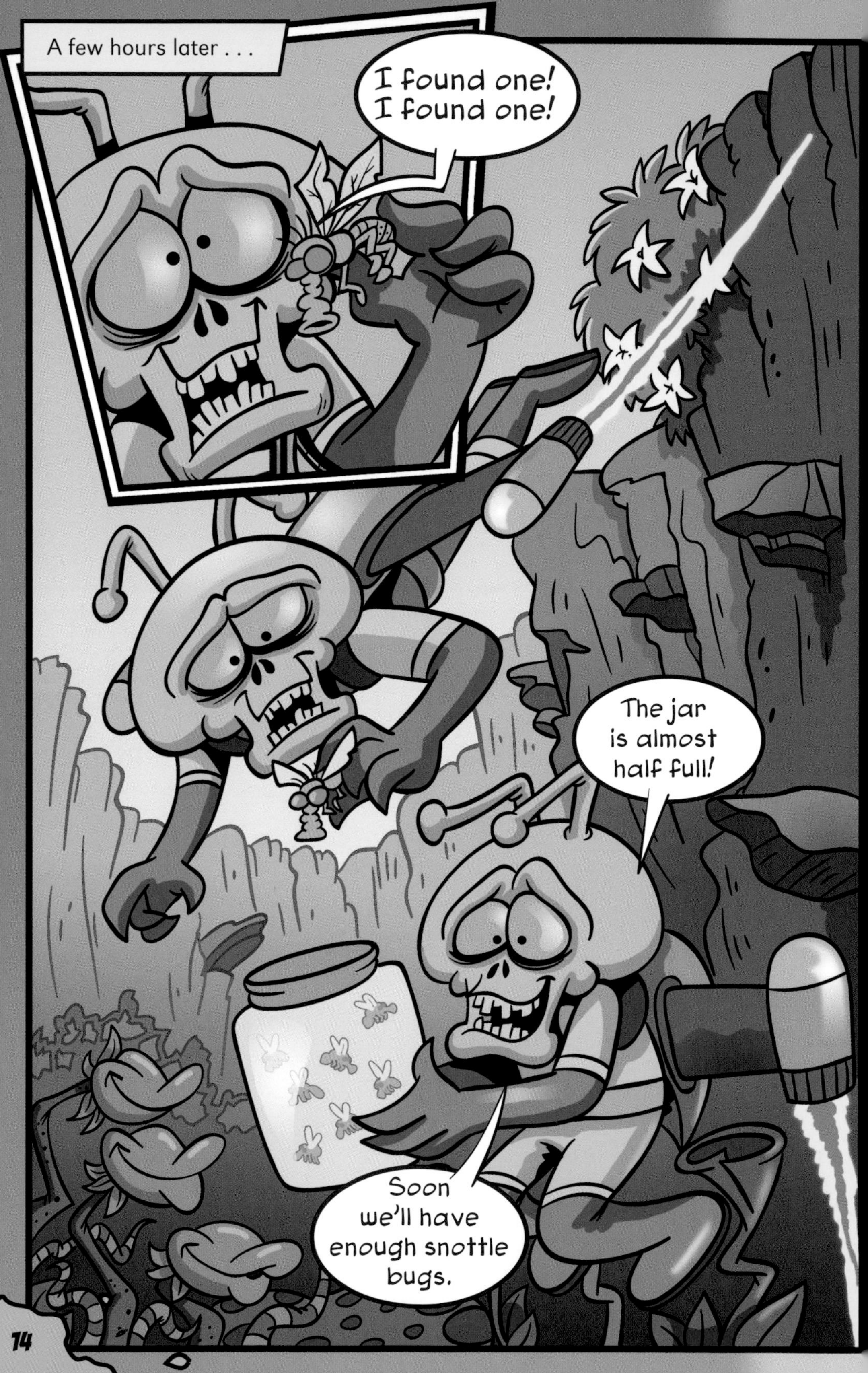
A few hours later . . .
I found one! I found one!
The jar is almost half full!
Soon we'll have enough snottle bugs.

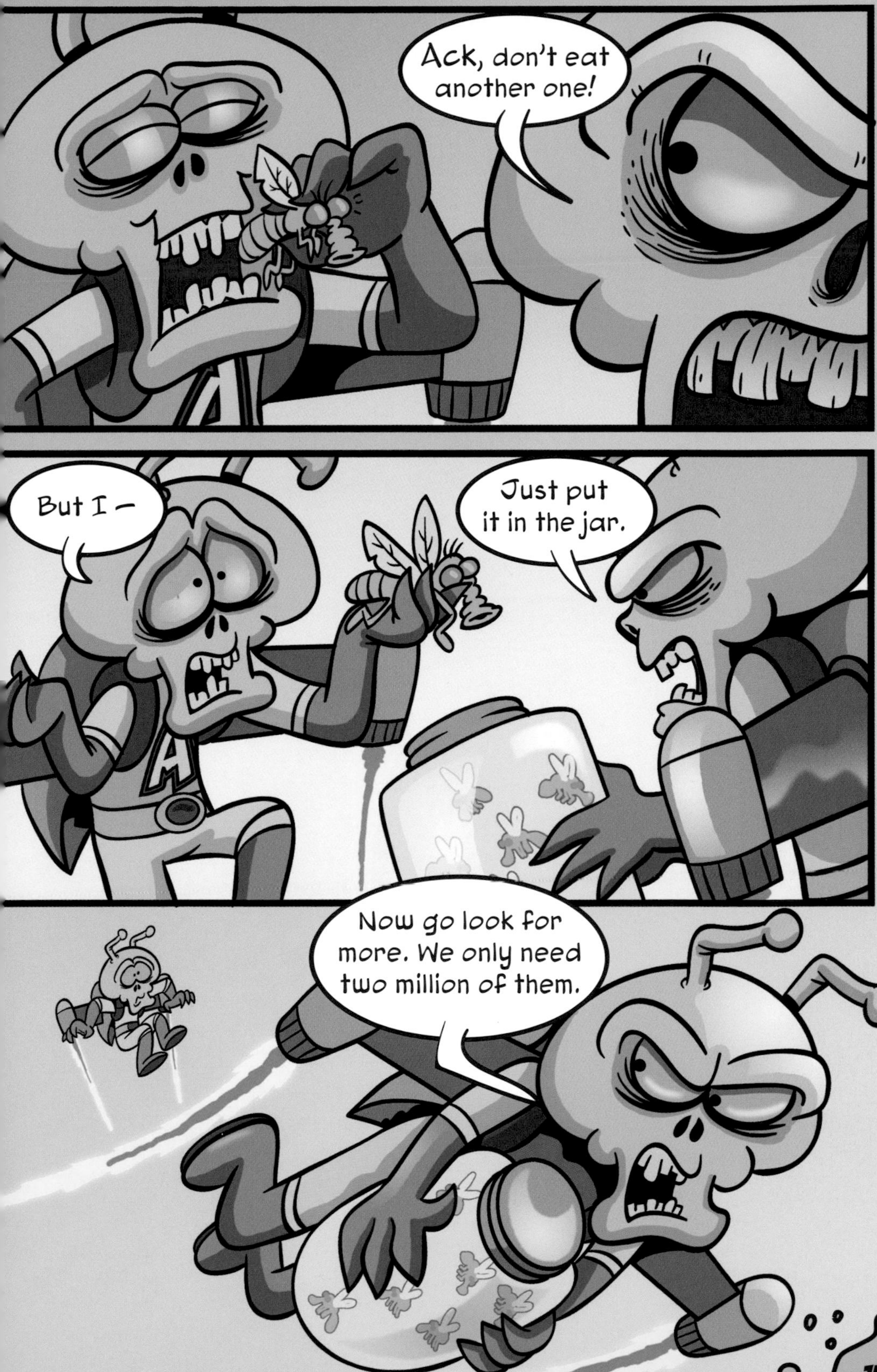
Ack, don't eat another one!
But I –
Just put it in the jar.
Now go look for more. We only need two million of them.

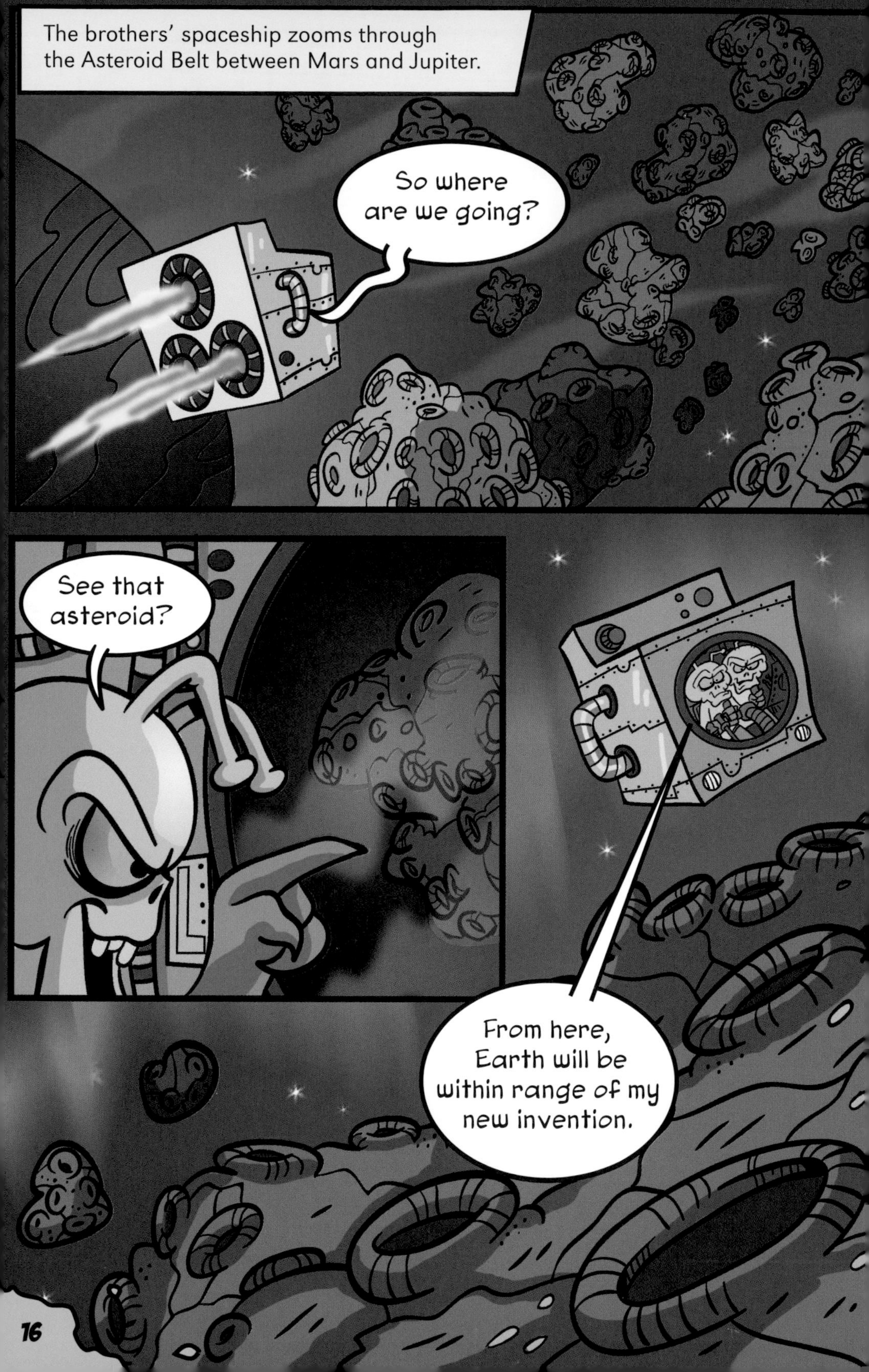
The brothers' spaceship zooms through the Asteroid Belt between Mars and Jupiter.
So where are we going?
See that asteroid?
From here, Earth will be within range of my new invention.

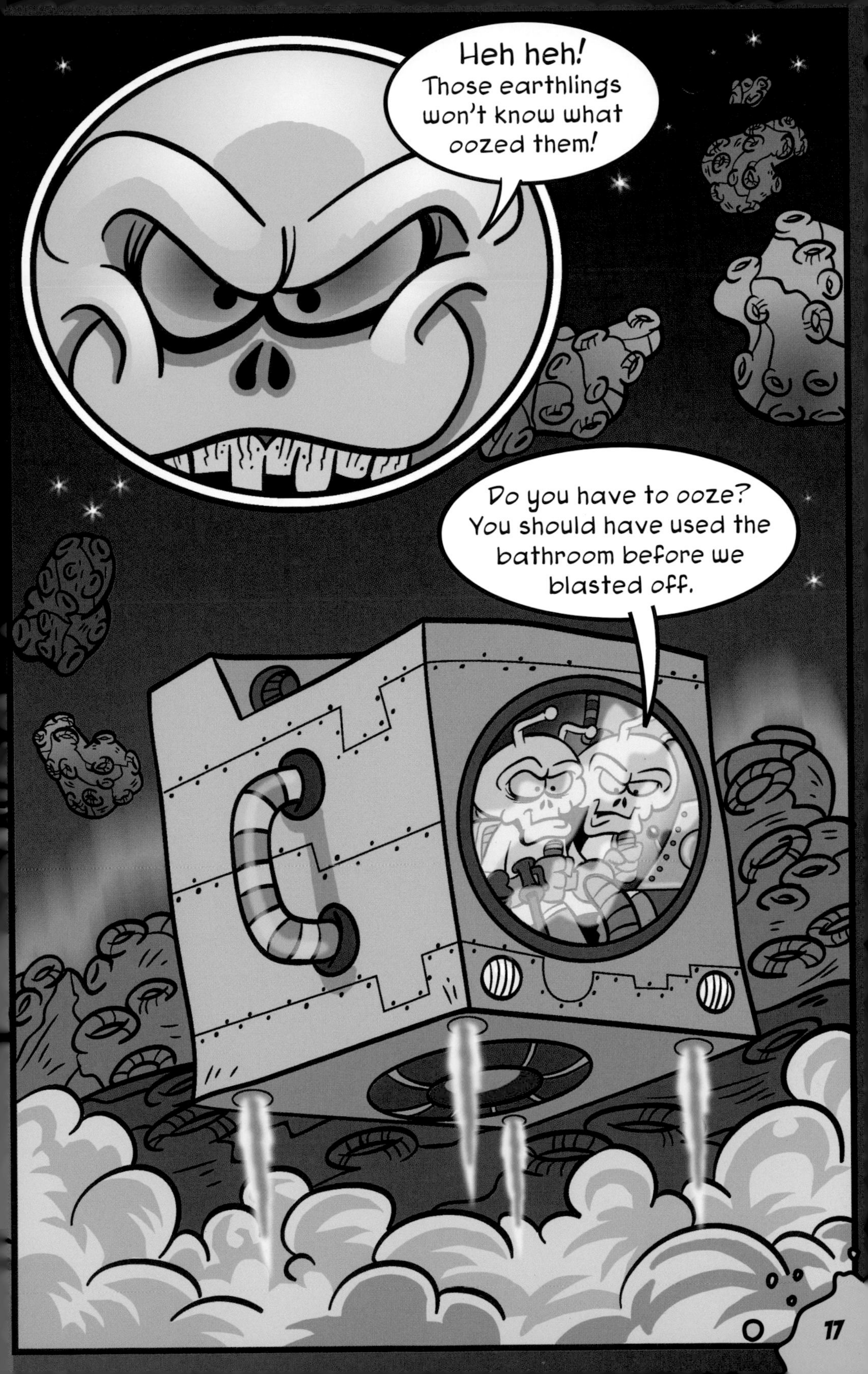
Heh heh! Those earthlings won't know what oozed them!
Do you have to ooze? You should have used the bathroom before we blasted off.

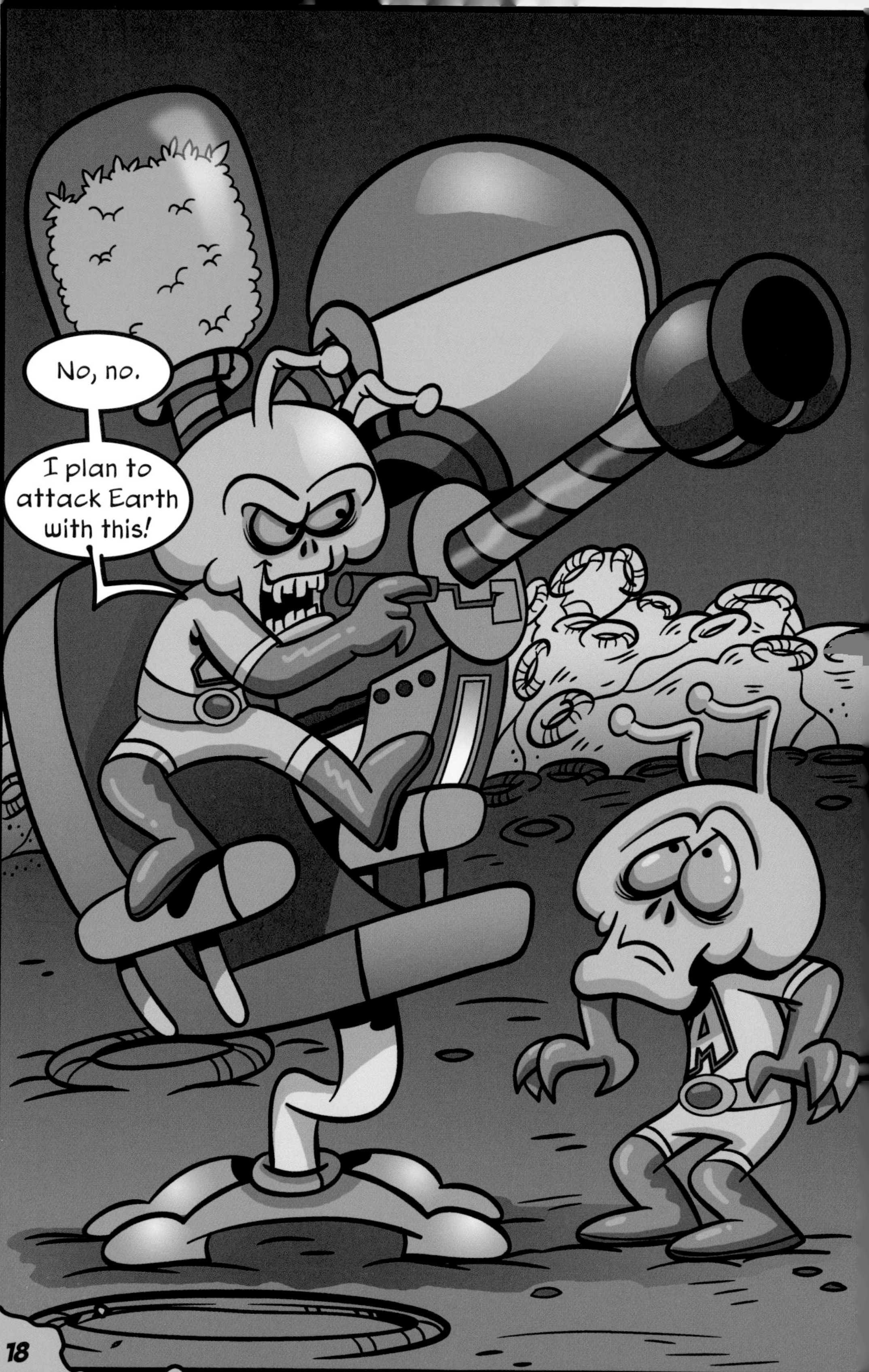
No, no.
I plan to attack Earth with this!

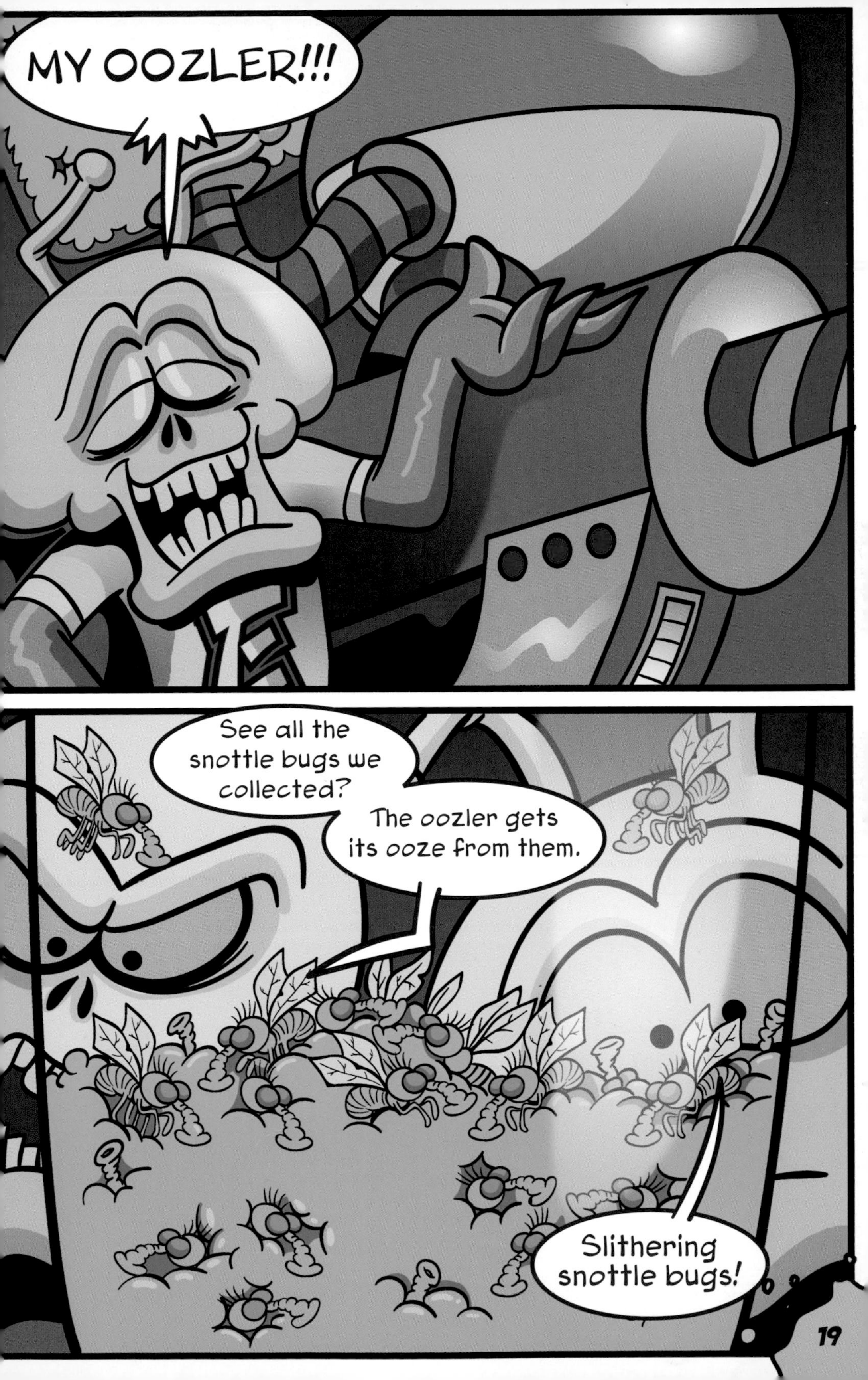
MY OOZLER!!!
See all the snottle bugs we collected?
The oozler gets its ooze from them.
Slithering snottle bugs!

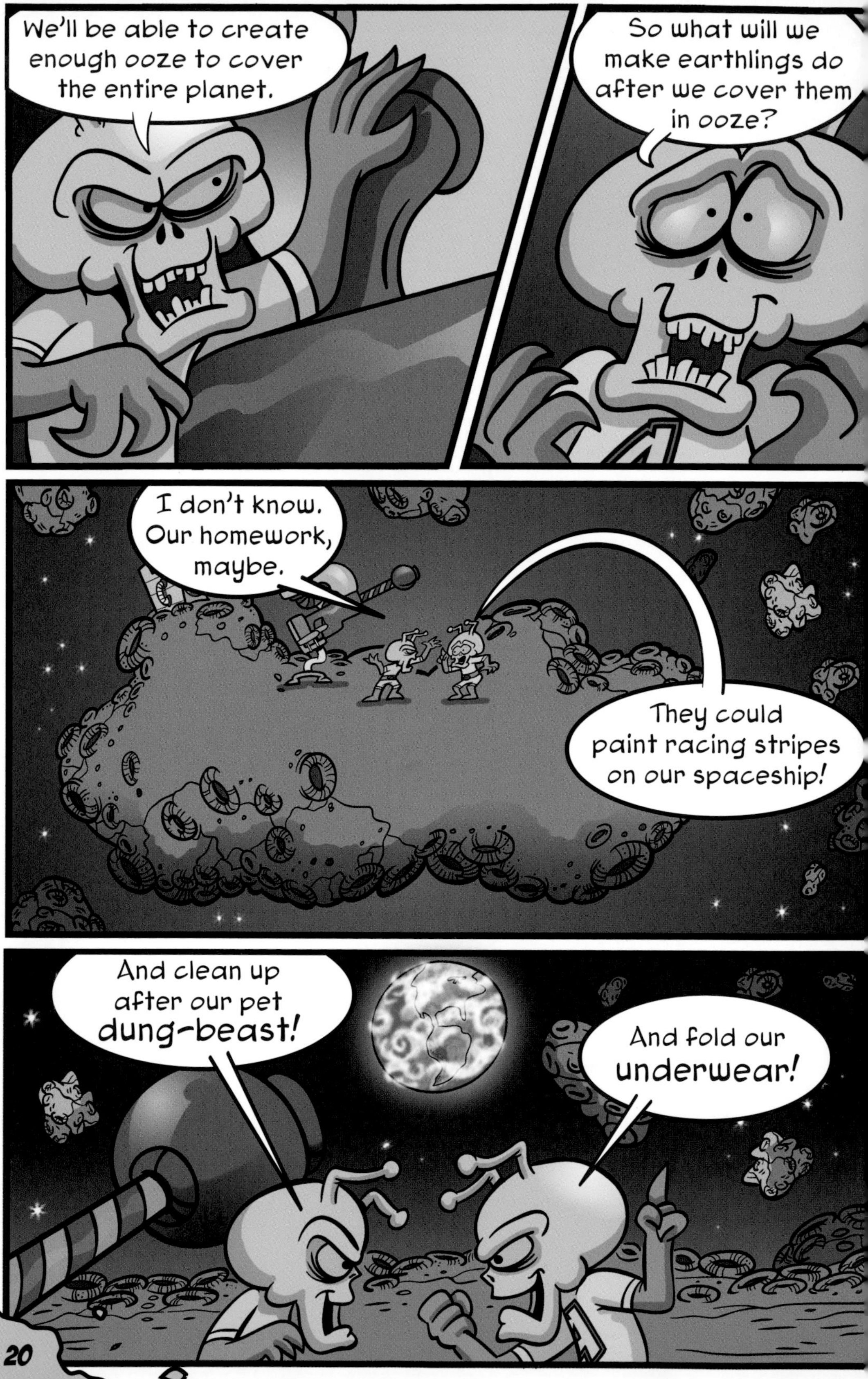
We'll be able to create enough ooze to cover the entire planet.
So what will we make earthlings do after we cover them in ooze?
I don't know. Our homework, maybe.
They could paint racing stripes on our spaceship!
And clean up after our pet dung-beast!
And fold our underwear!

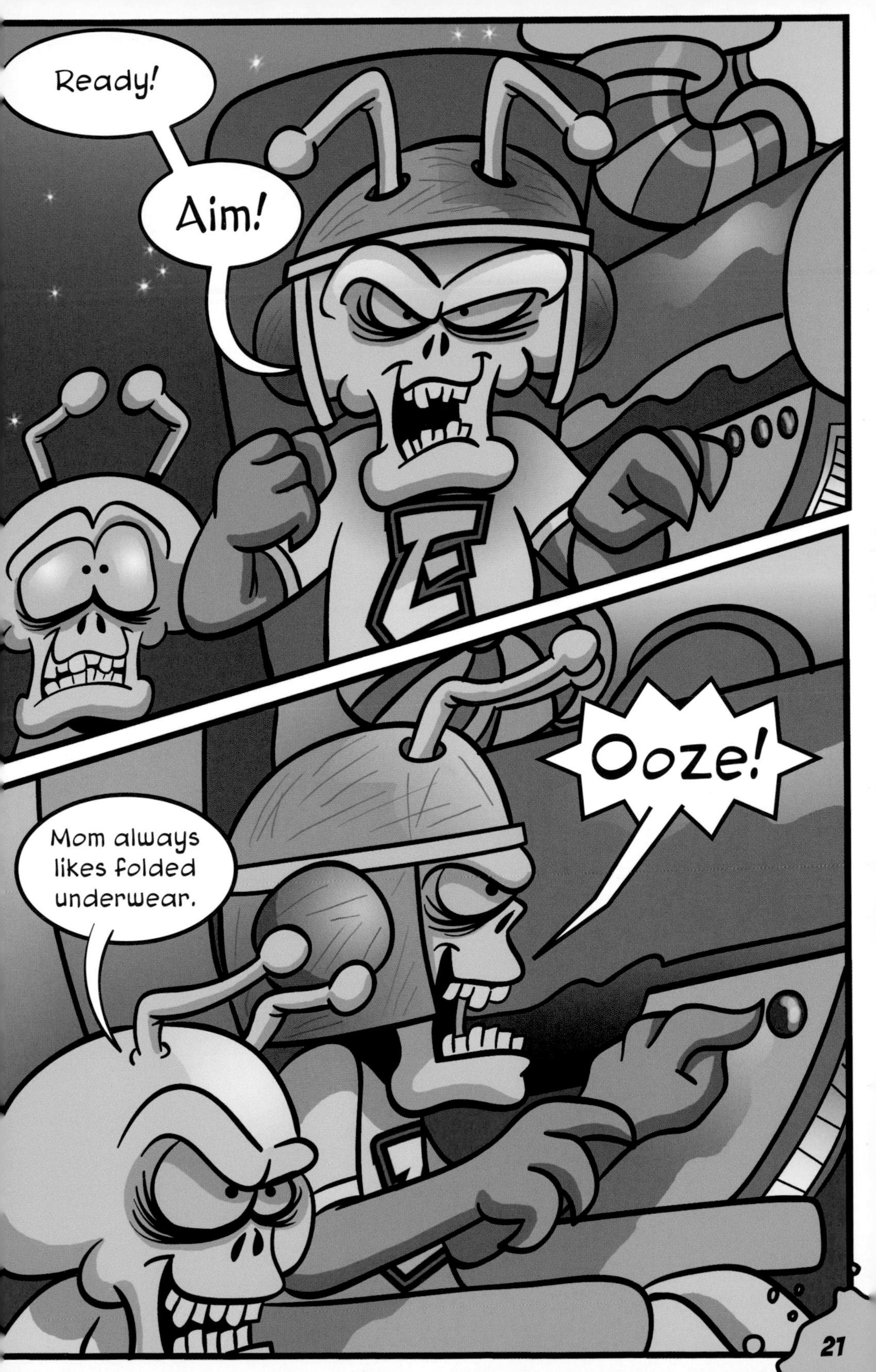
Ready!
Aim!
Mom always likes folded underwear.
Ooze!

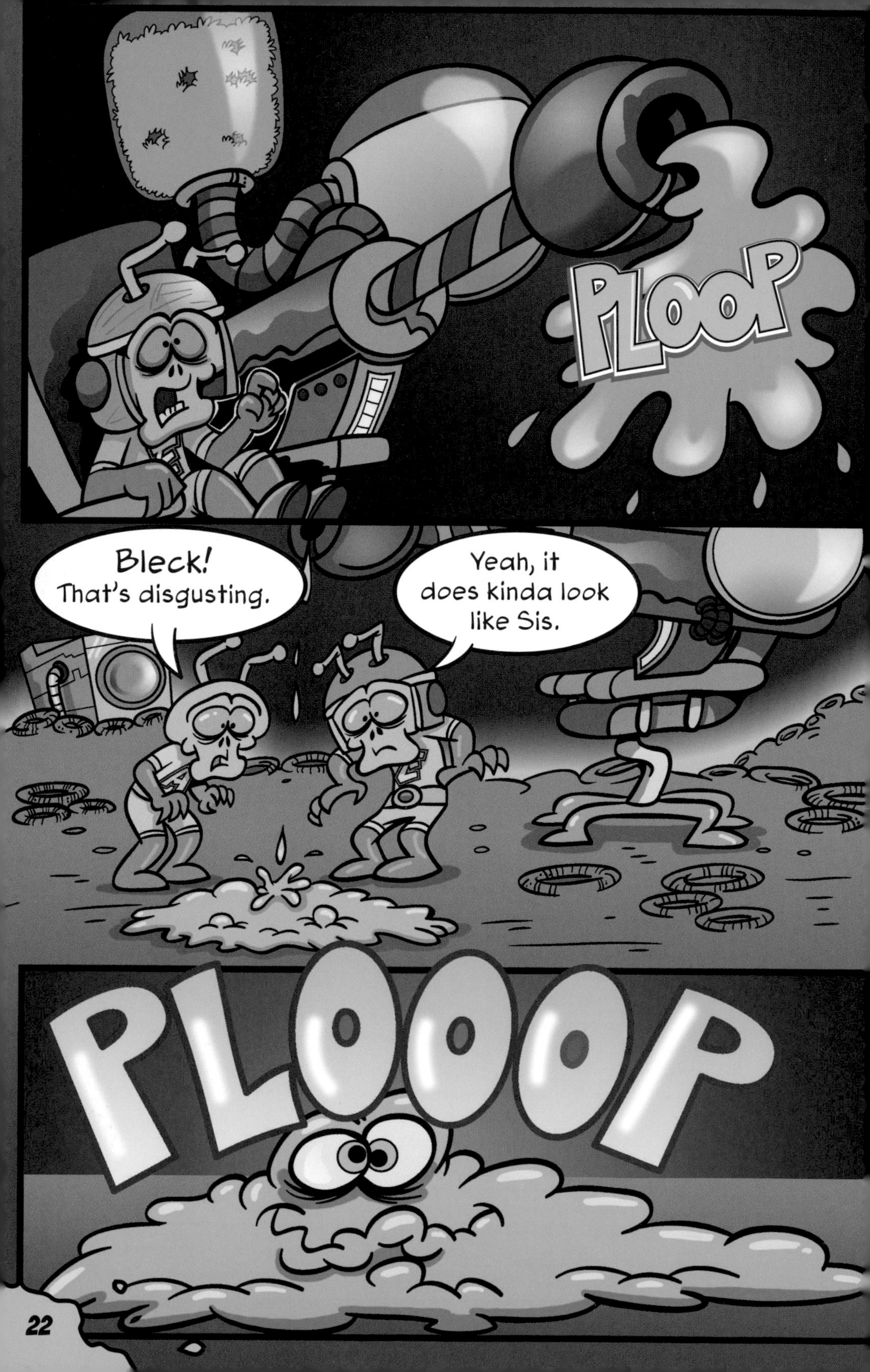
PLOOP
Bleck! That's disgusting.
Yeah, it does kinda look like Sis.
PLOOOP

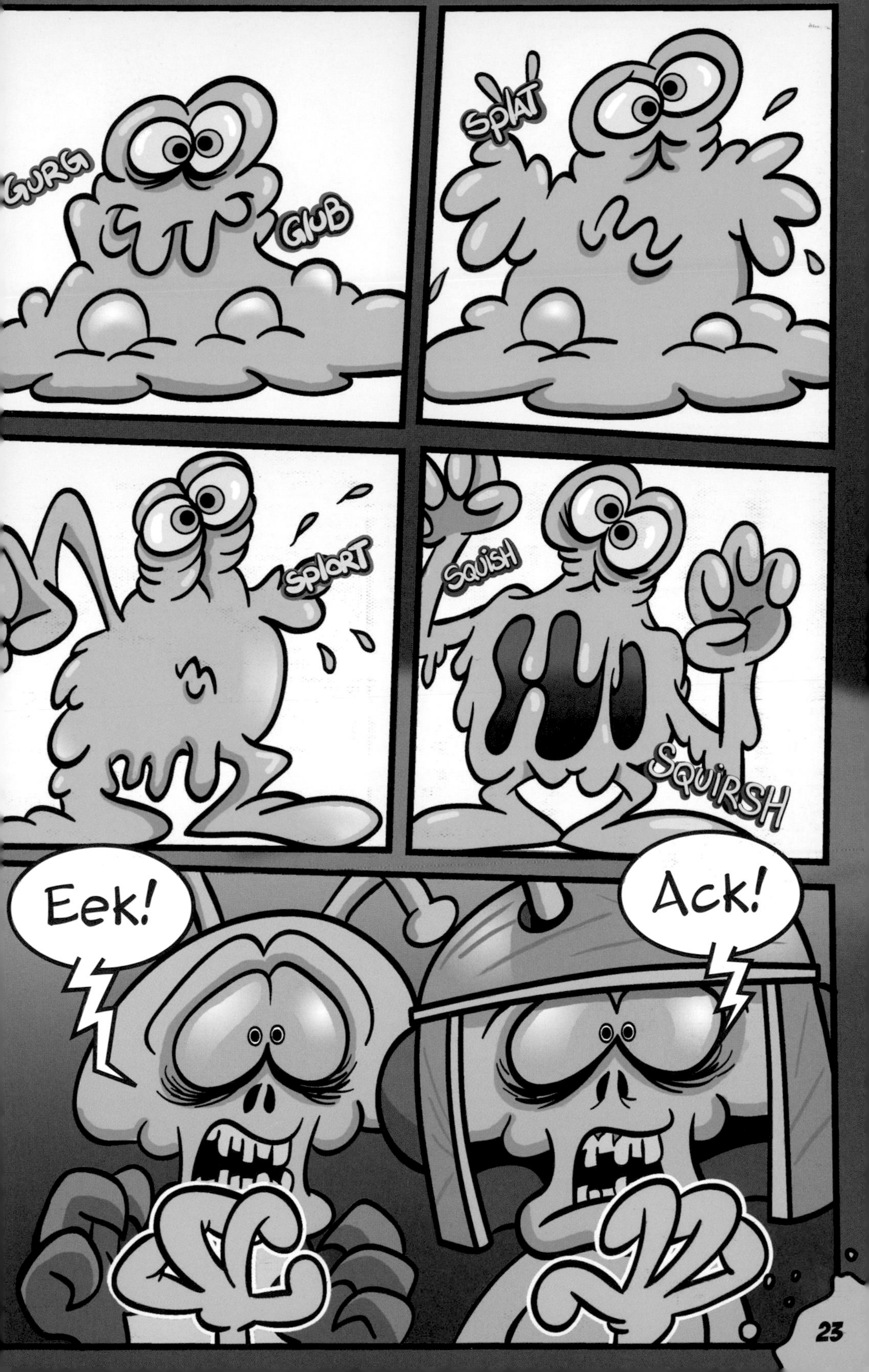
GURG
GLUB
SPLAT
SPLORT
SQUISH
SQUIRSH
Eek!
Ack!

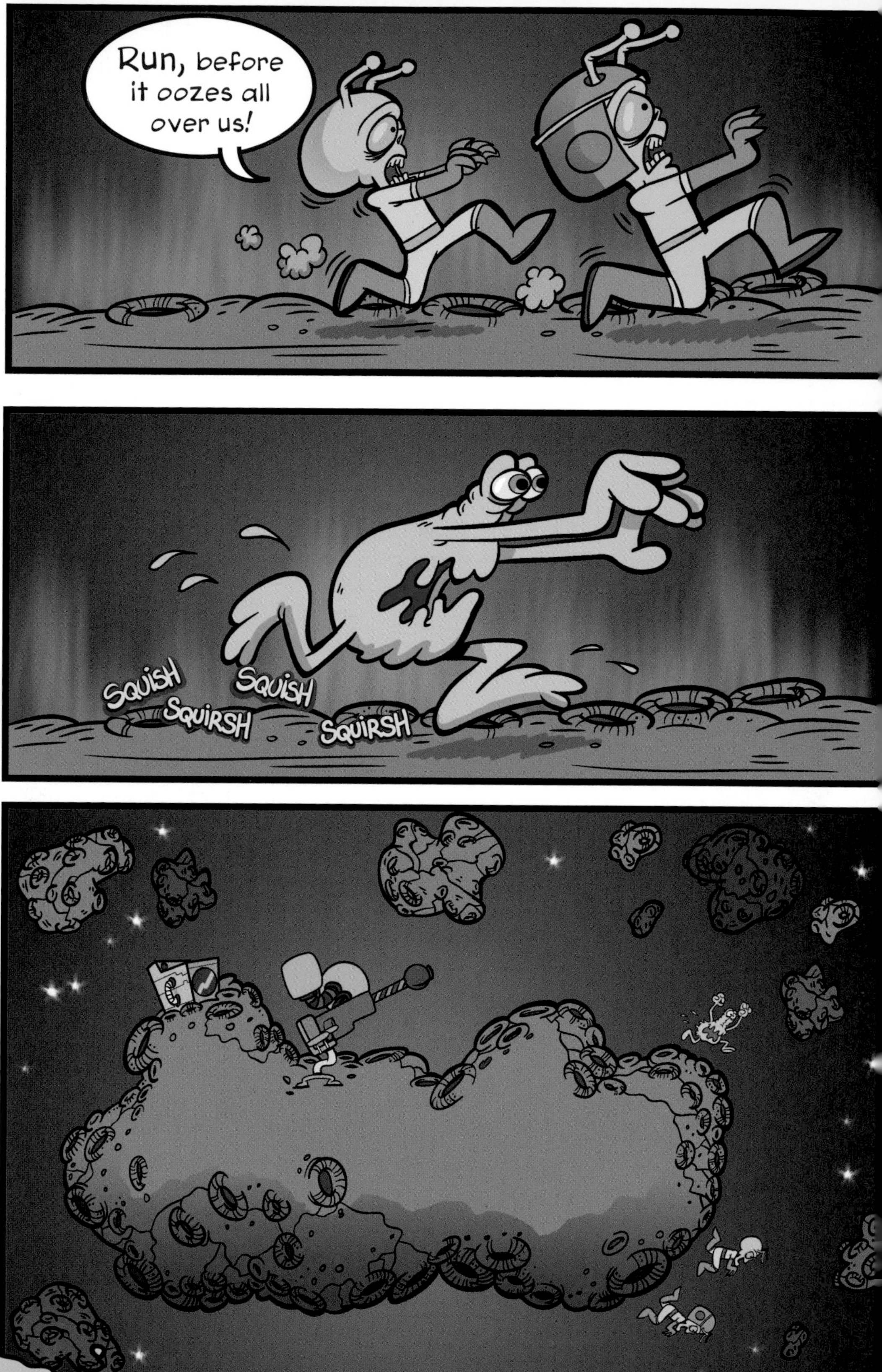
Run, before it oozes all over us!
SQUISH
SQUIRSH
SQUISH
SQUIRSH

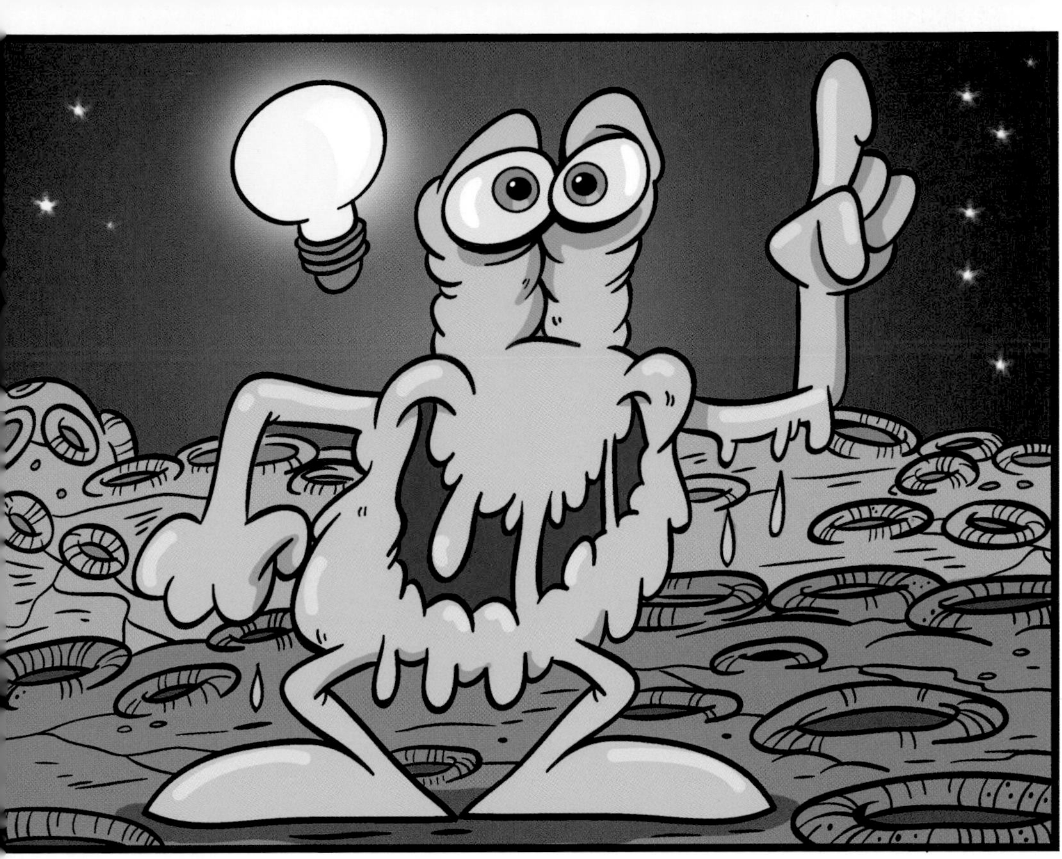

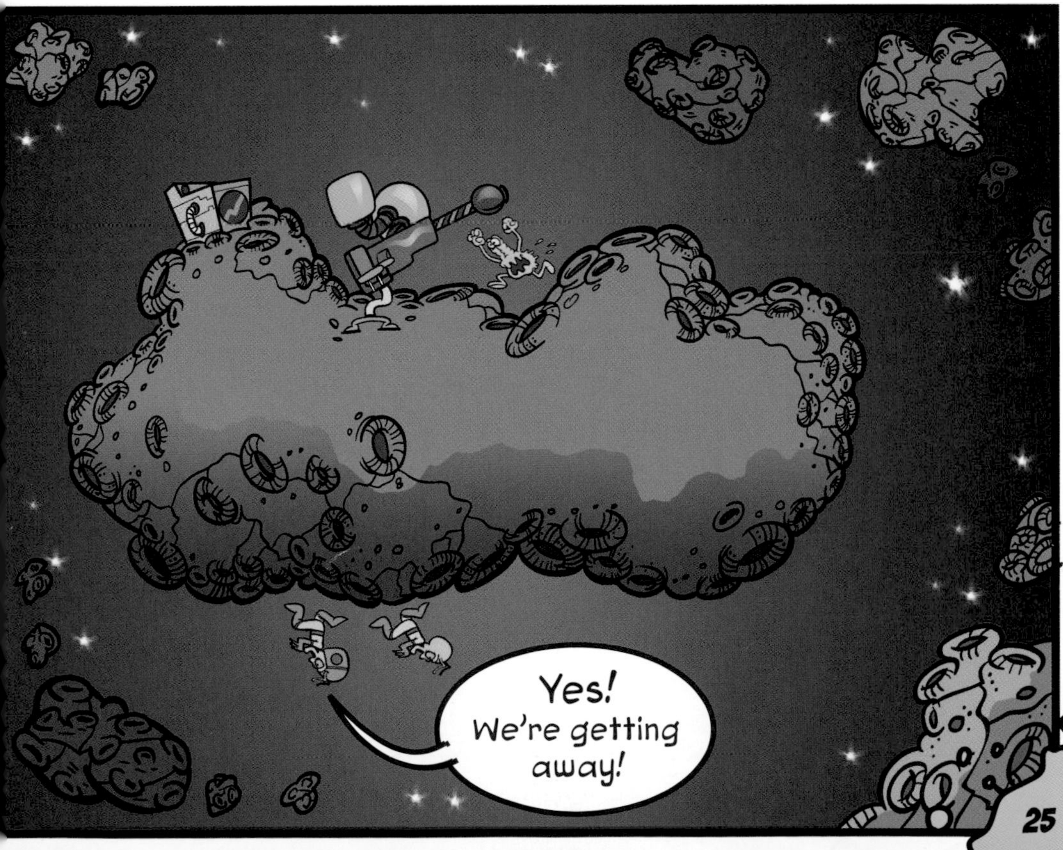
Yes!
We're getting away!

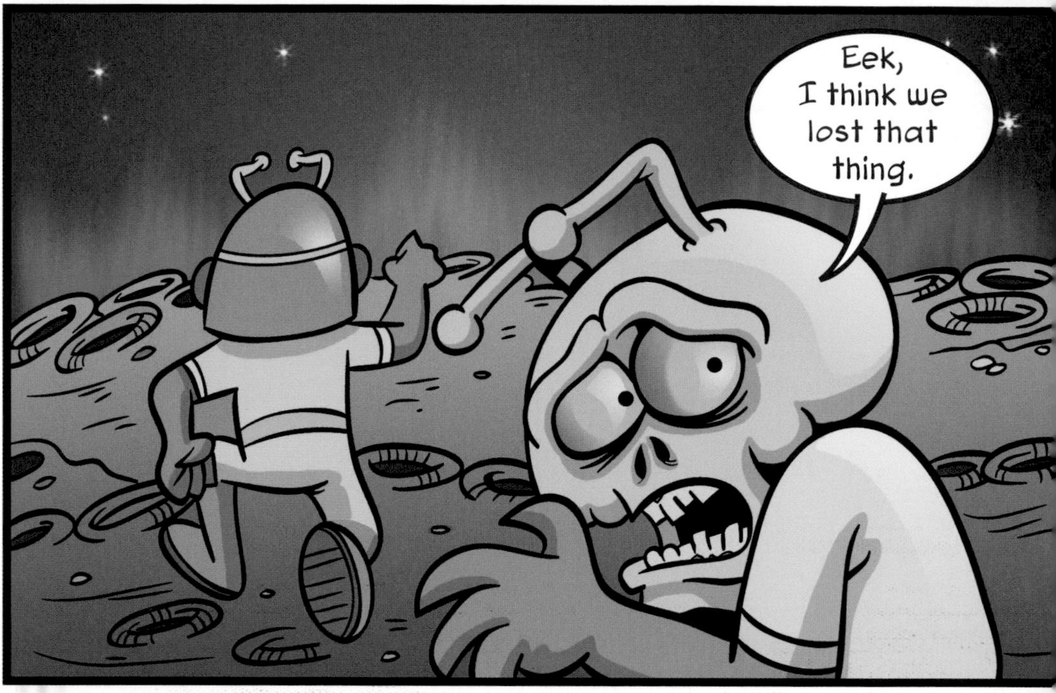
Eek,
I think we
lost that
thing.

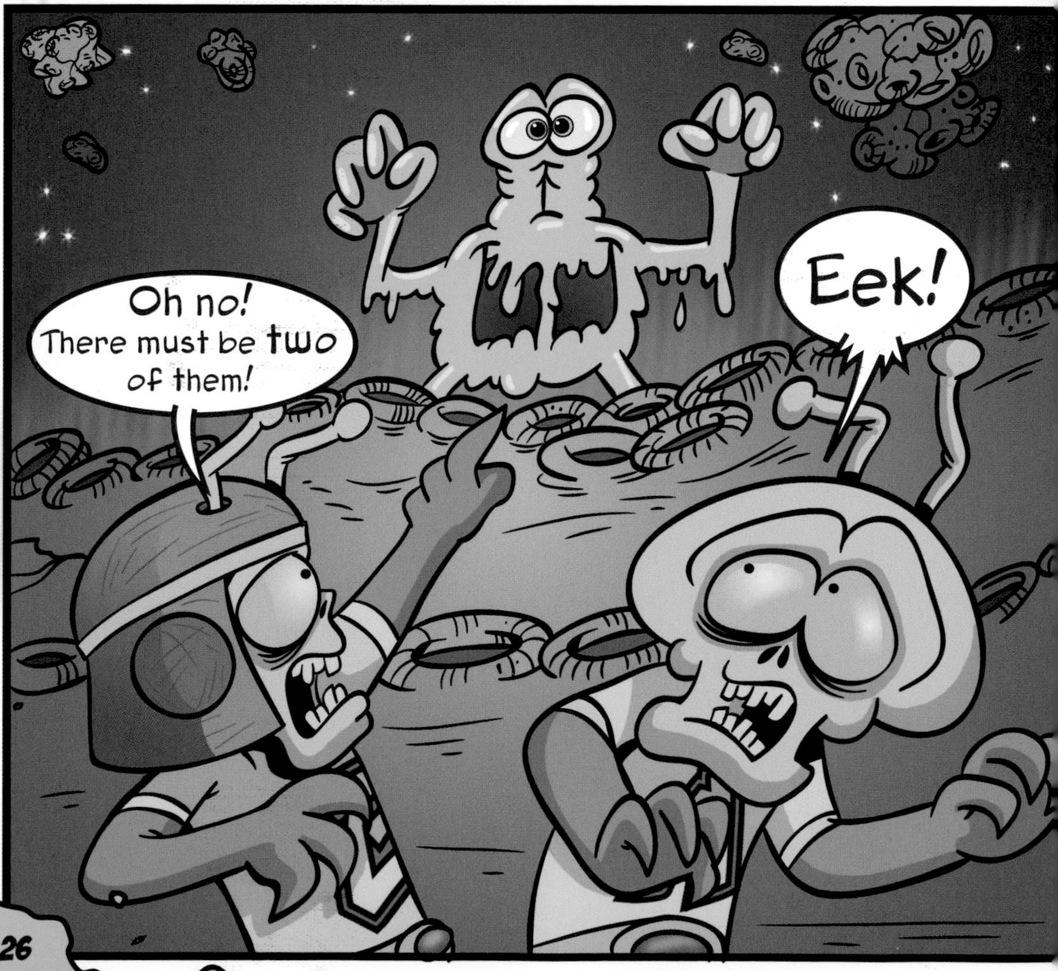
Oh no!
There must be two
of them!
Eek!

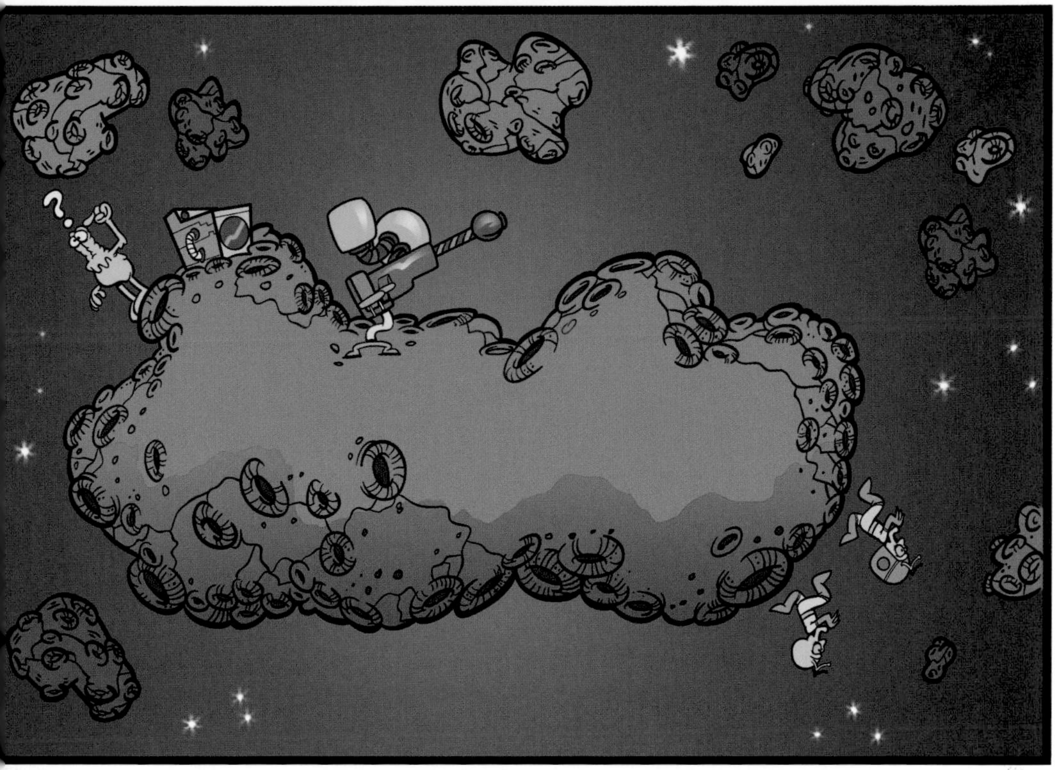
?

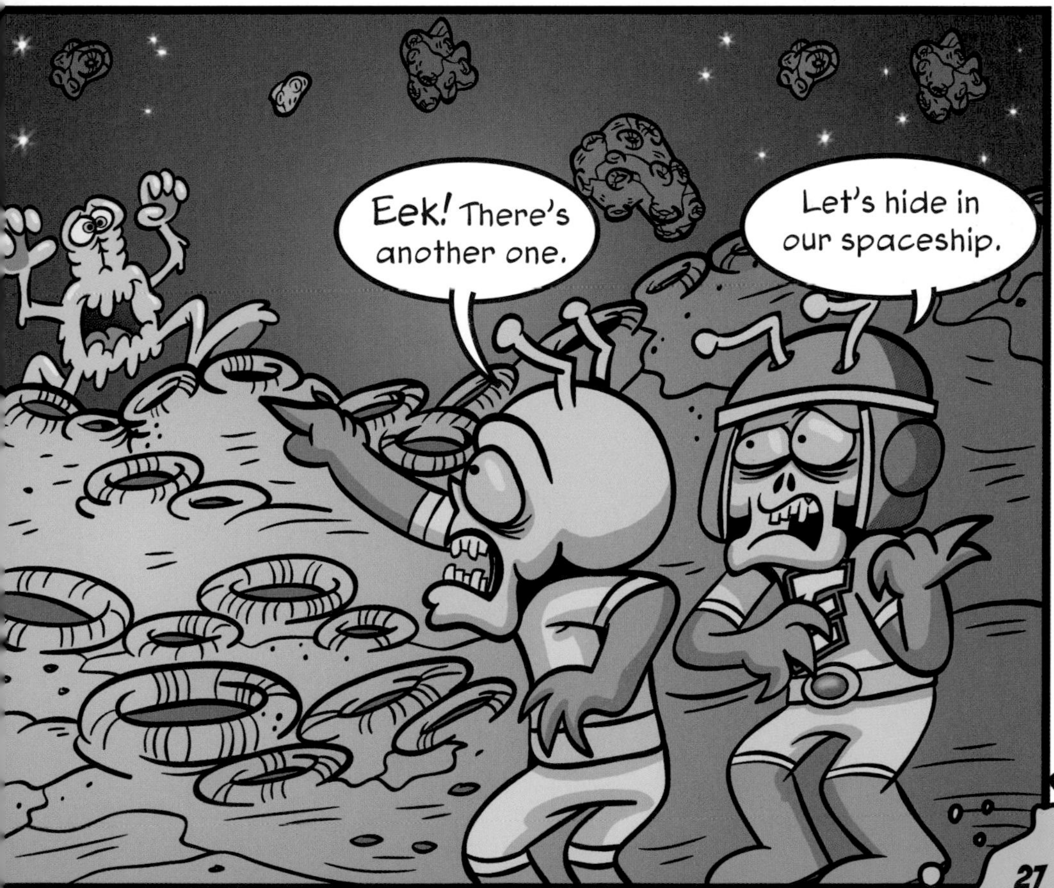
Eek! There's another one.
Let's hide in our spaceship.

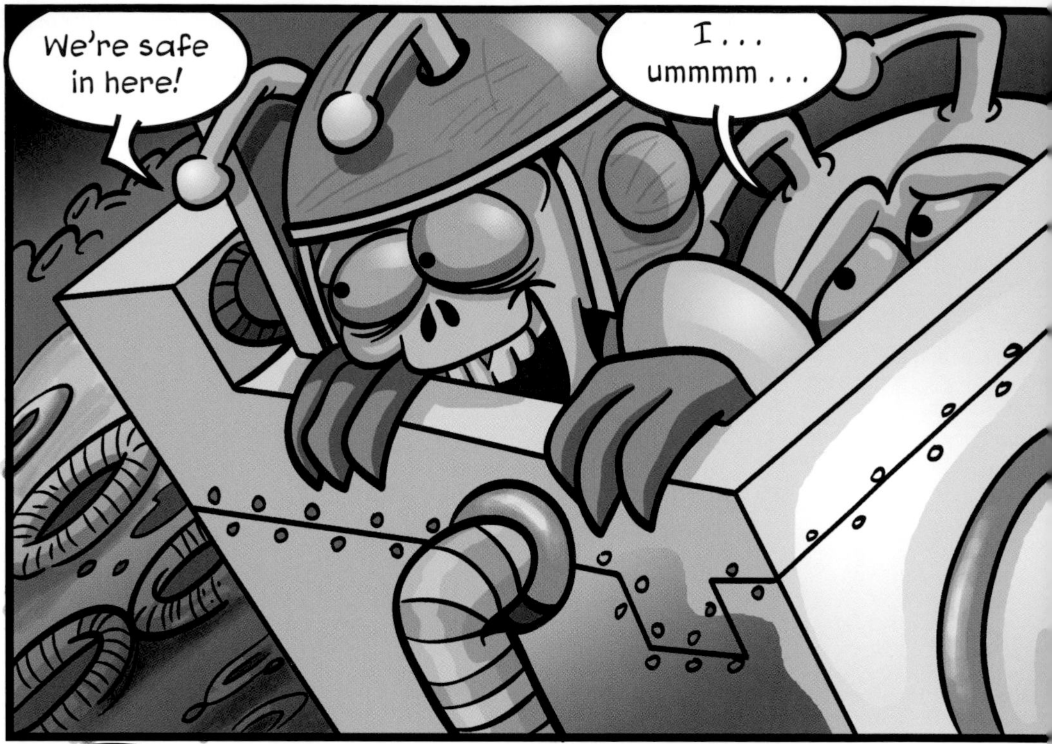
We're safe in here!
I . . . ummmm . . .

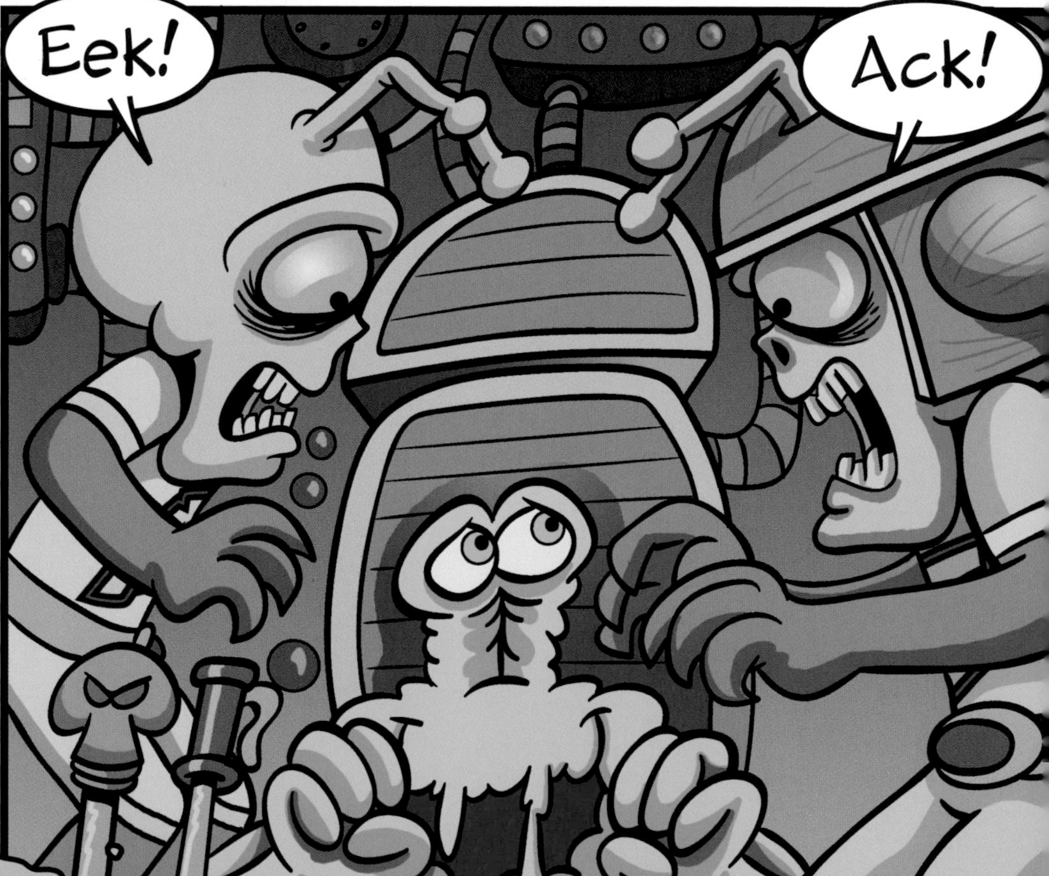
Eek!
Ack!

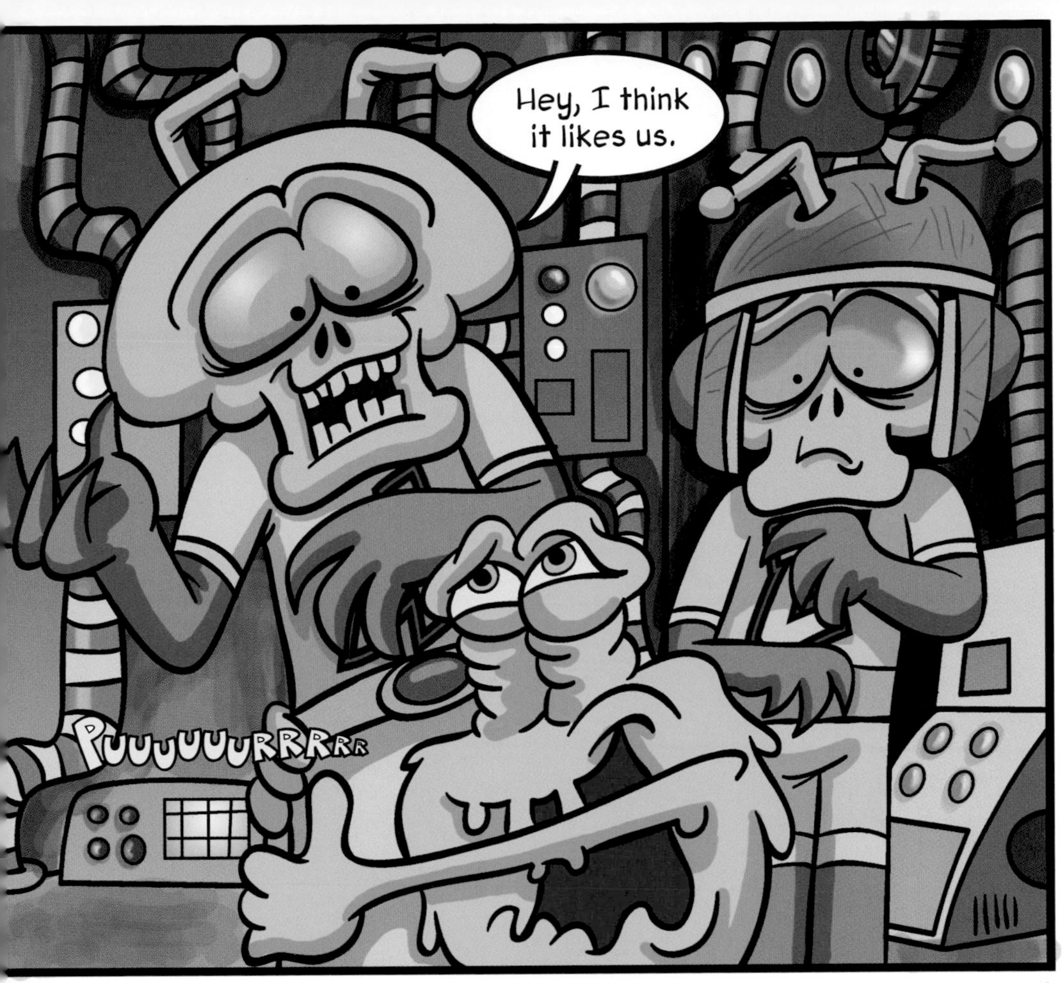
Hey, I think it likes us.
PUUUUUURRRRR

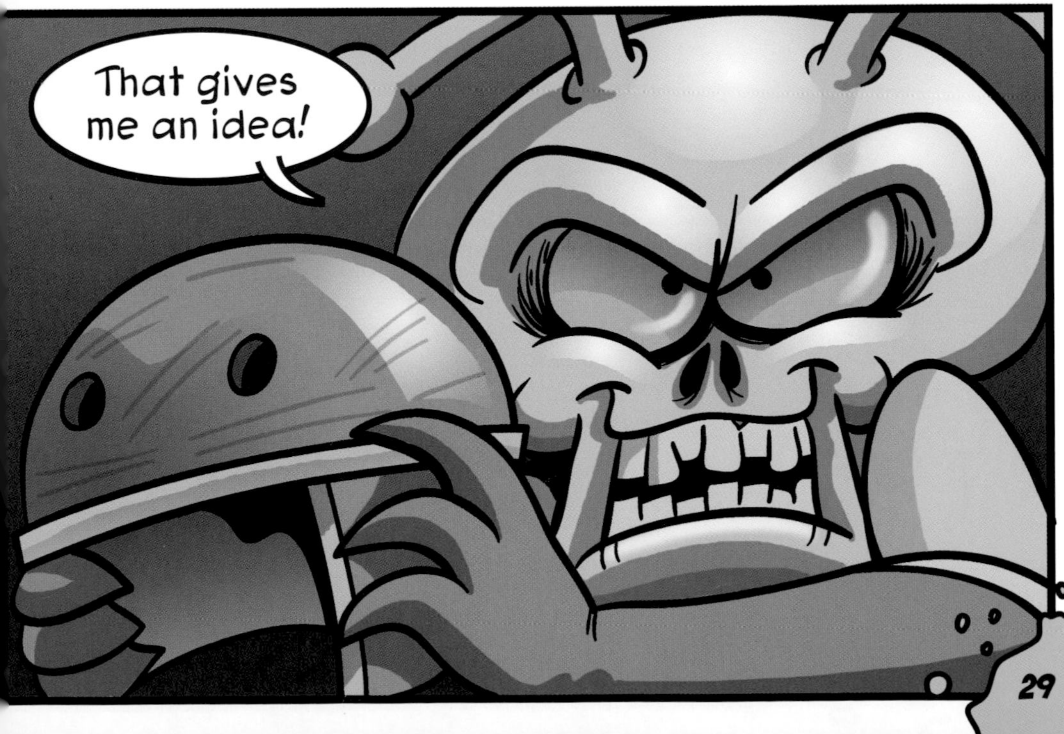
That gives me an idea!

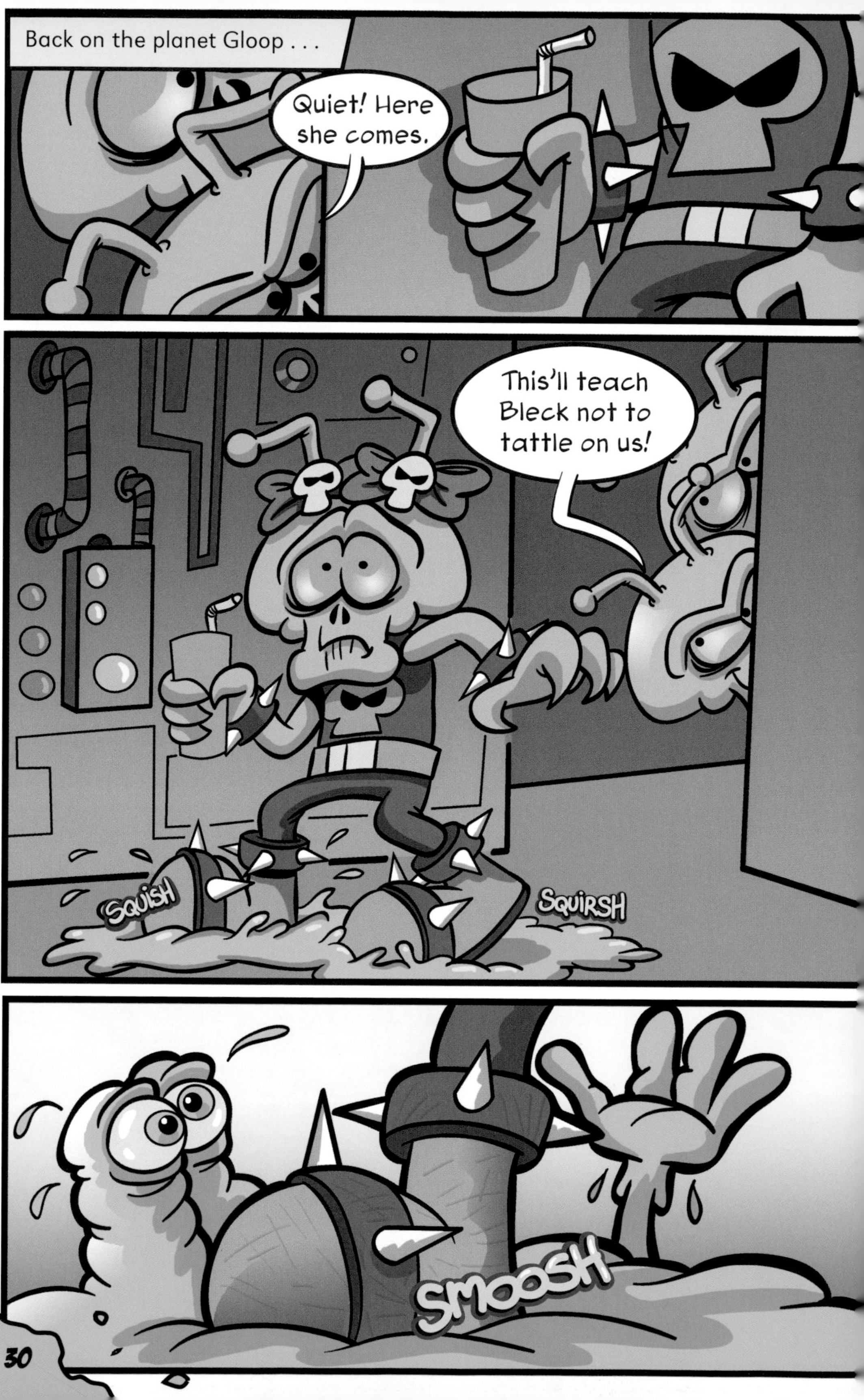
Back on the planet Gloop . . .
Quiet! Here she comes.
This'll teach Bleck not to tattle on us!
SQUISH
SQUIRSH
SMOOSH

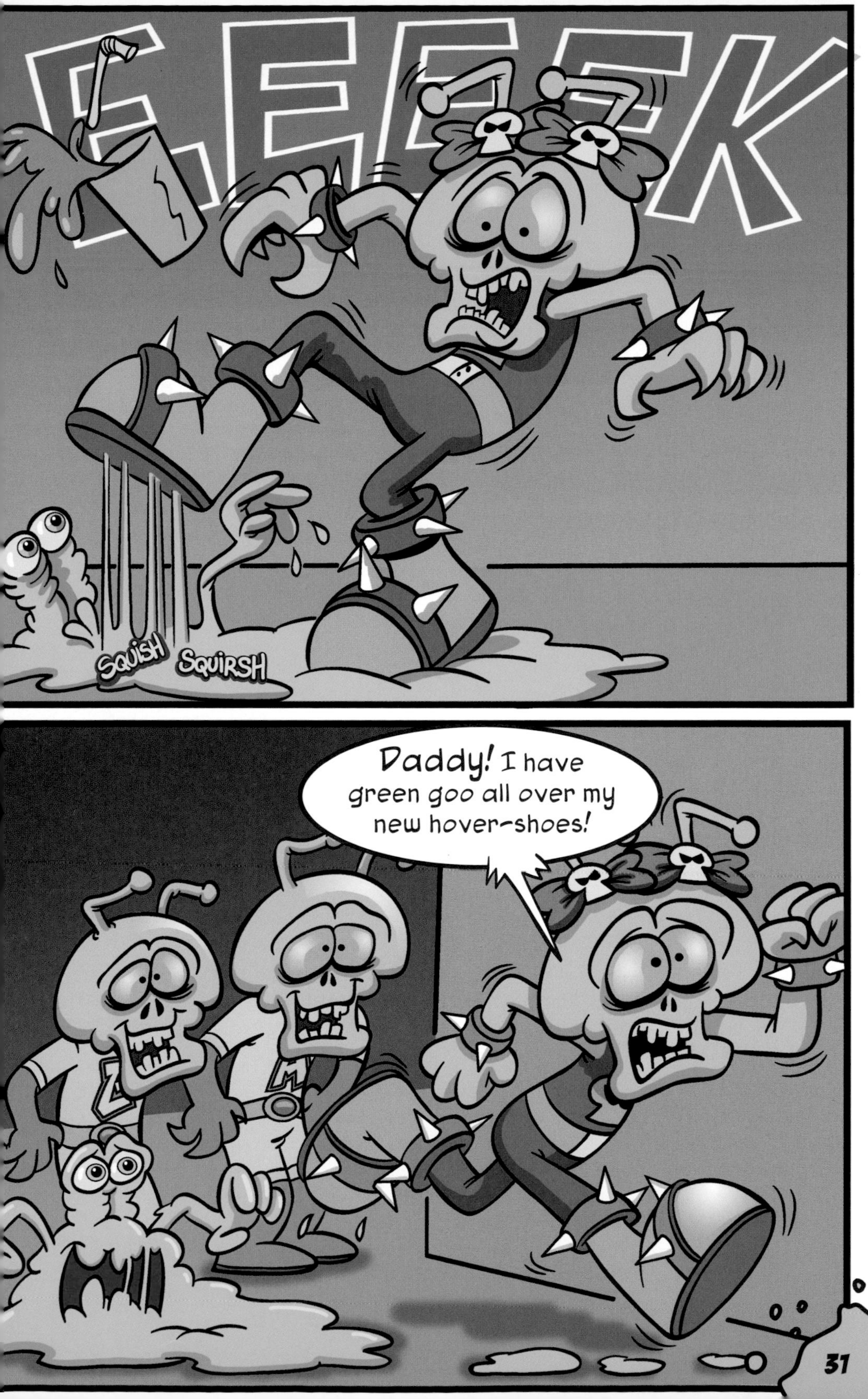
EEEEK
SQUISH
SQUIRSH
Daddy! I have green goo all over my new hover-shoes!

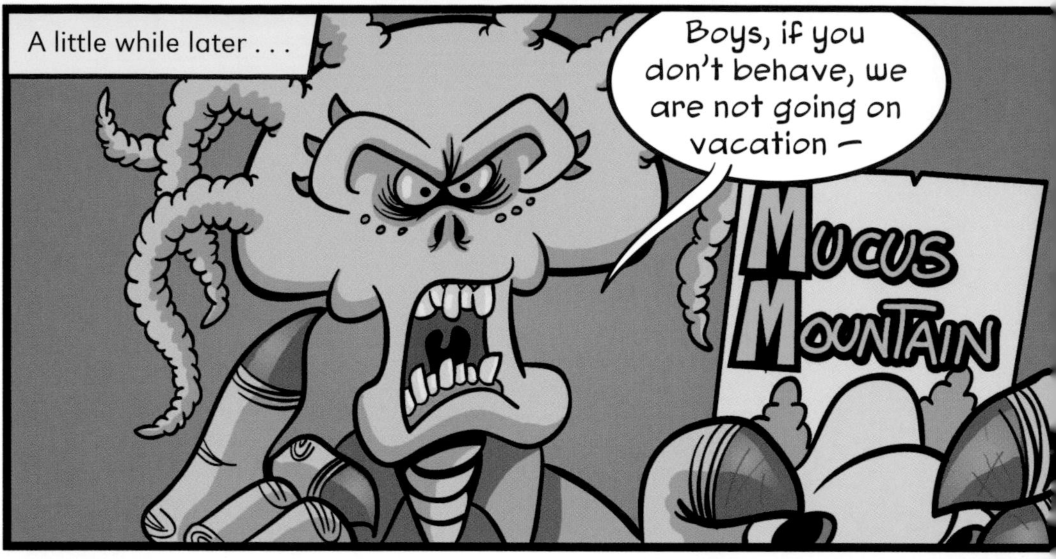
A little while later . . .
Boys, if you don't behave, we are not going on vacation –
MUCUS MOUNTAIN

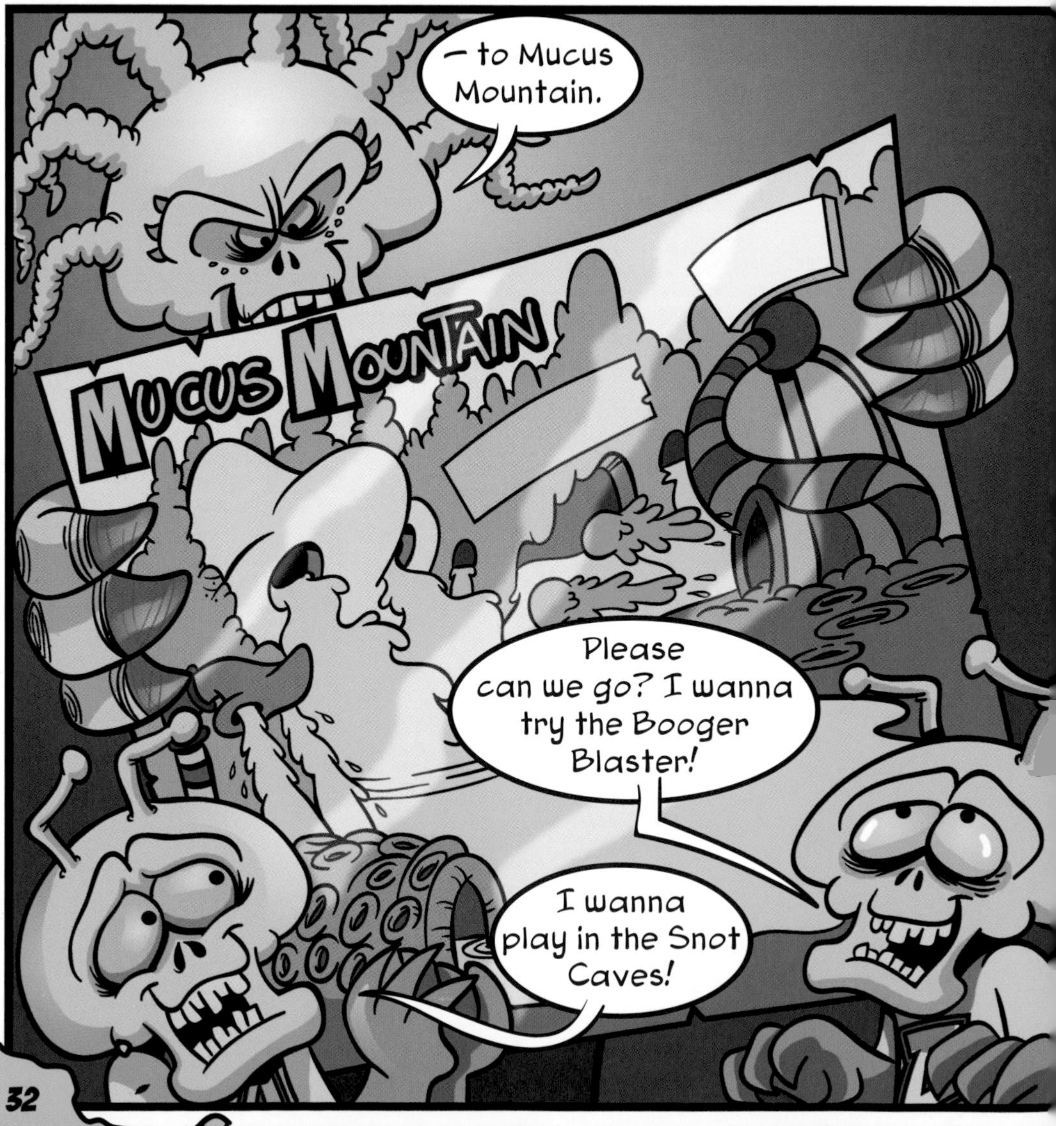
– to Mucus Mountain.
MUCUS MOUNTAIN
Please can we go? I wanna try the Booger Blaster!
I wanna play in the Snot Caves!

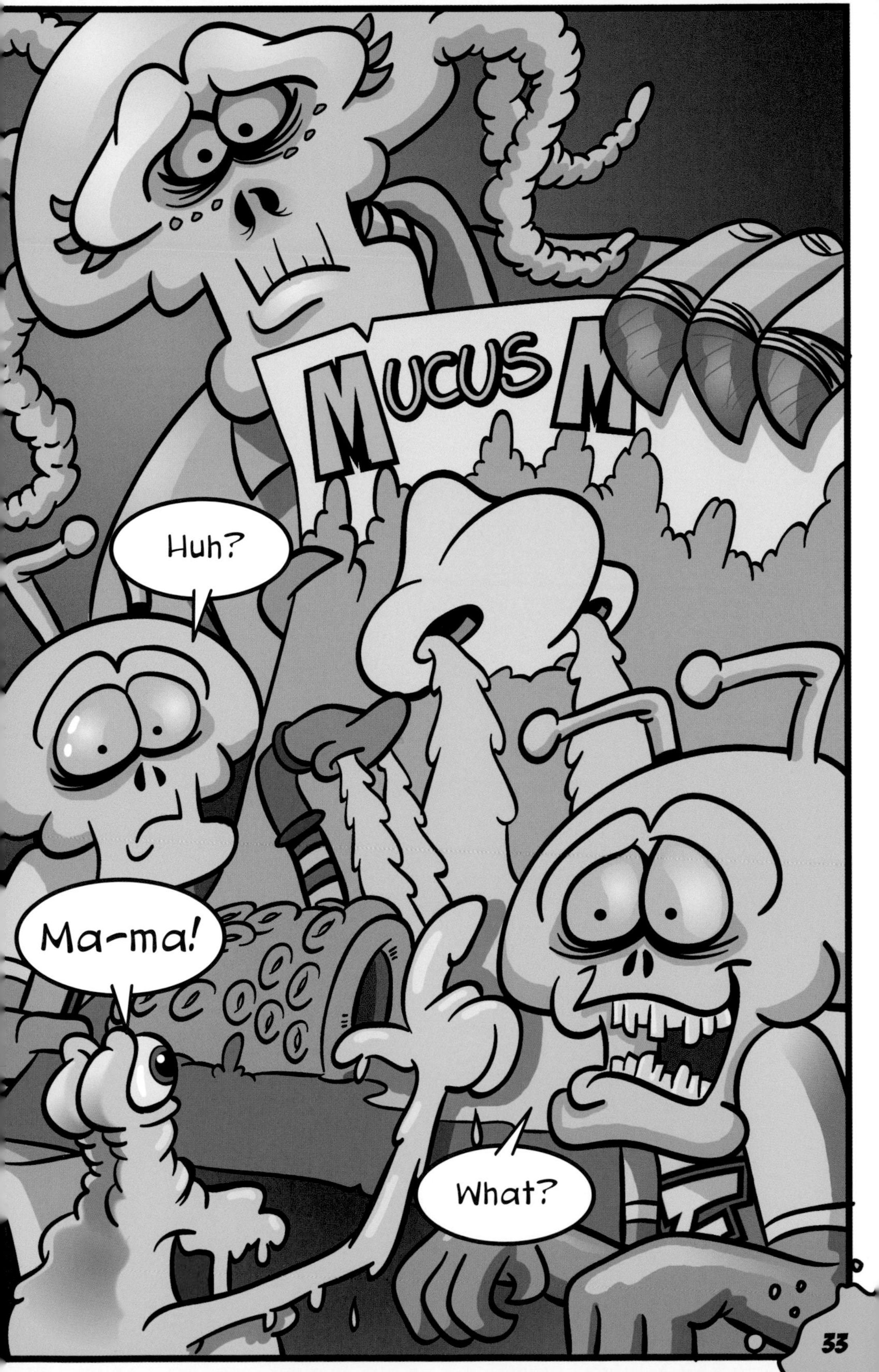
MUCUS M
Huh?
Ma-ma!
What?

ABOUT THE AUTHOR

Blake A. Hoena once spent a whole weekend just watching his favorite science-fiction movies. Those movies made him wonder what kind of aliens, with their death rays and hyper-drives, couldn't actually conquer Earth. That's when he created Eek and Ack, who play at conquering Earth like earthling kids play at stopping bad guys. Blake has written more than twenty books for children, and currently lives in Roseville, Minnesota.

ABOUT THE ILLUSTRATOR

Steve Harpster has loved to draw funny cartoons, mean monsters, and goofy gadgets since he was able to pick up a pencil. In first grade, he was able to avoid his writing assignments by working on the pictures for stories instead. Steve was able to land a job drawing funny pictures for books, and that's really what he's best at. Steve lives in Columbus, Ohio, with his wonderful wife, Karen, and their sheepdog, Doodle.

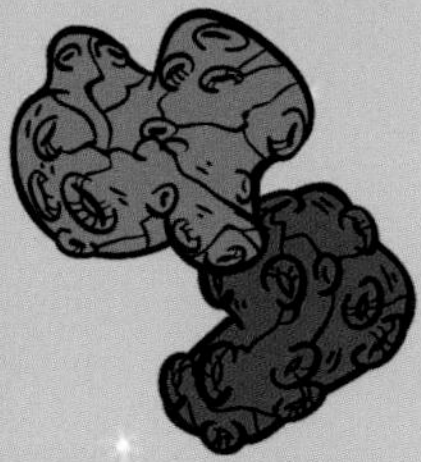

GLOSSARY

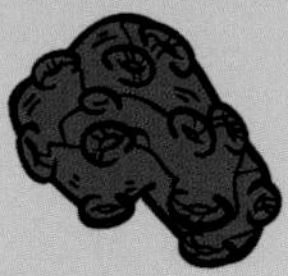

asteroid (AS-tuh-royd)—a large rock floating in outer space; some asteroids are found between Mars and Jupiter in an area known as the asteroid belt.

observatory (uhb-ZUR-vuh-tor-ee)—a building used to study stars and the sky with telescopes and other scientific instruments

sinister plot (SIN-iss-tur PLAHT)—an evil plan, such as a plan to destroy Earth

telescope (TEL-uh-skope)—an instrument that makes things that are very far away seem closer and larger; telescopes are used to study stars and planets.

vaporize (VAY-pur-eyez)—to destroy something by turning it into smaller pieces or into dust

EEK AND ACK'S GALAXY OF FACTS

Scientists call that sticky stuff in your nose "mucus." It's also known as snot, boogers, goobers, phlegm, and loogies.

There are four pairs of open spaces in your skull near your nose. The spaces are called "sinuses." Sinuses are snot factories where mucus is produced.

Your sinuses produce about one cup of mucus a day. Yuck!

Snot and boogers, along with your nose hairs, are like glue traps. They clean the air you breathe by trapping dirt and germs. Dirt and germs get stuck in the mucus before they get into your lungs.

Mucus is normally clear in color. It turns brown, yellow, or green because of the junk it traps and keeps from getting into your lungs.

Your mucus also turns green if you have a sinus infection.

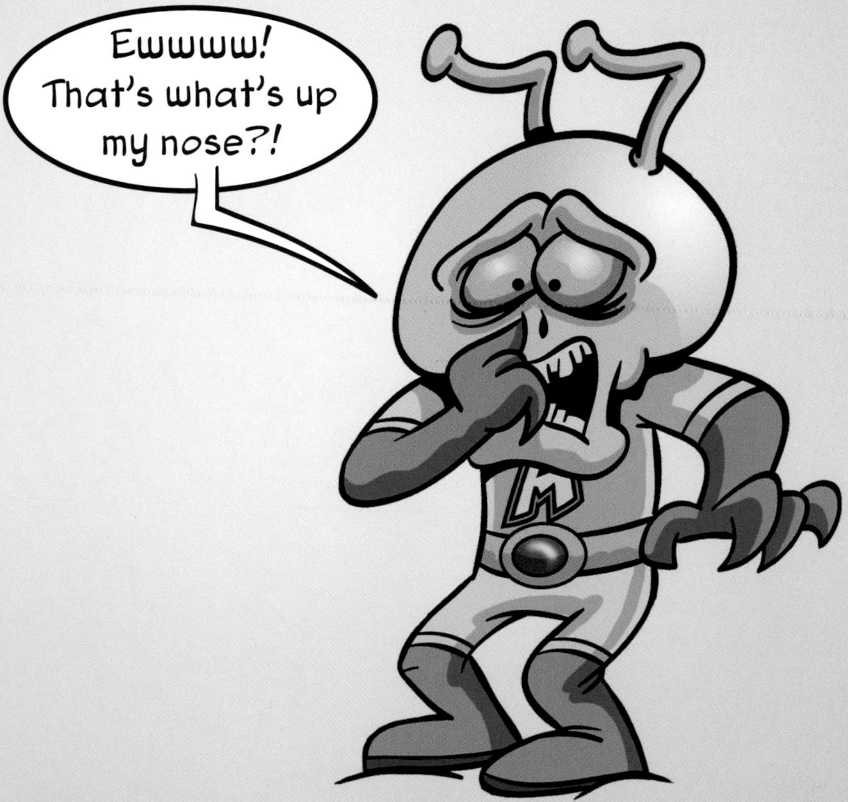
Ewwww! That's what's up my nose?!

DISCUSSION QUESTIONS

1. If Eek and Ack conquered Earth, which brother would you rather have bossing you around? Why? How are Eek and Ack different?

2. Eek and Ack want to make Earthlings do their chores. Do you have chores that you wish someone else would do? Why? Who would you make do them?

3. Eek and Ack's plan to conquer Earth doesn't work the way they wanted it to. Did that bother them? Do plans always have to turn out the way you want them to? Why or why not?